BETWEEN TWO SEAS

A SHORT STORY COLLECTION

CERECE RENNIE MURPHY

LionSky
PUBLISHING

Cover Illustration: Hilary Wilson

Cover Design: Anansi & Hayes

Print Design & Typesetting: Anansi & Hayes

Author Photo: Kea Taylor, Imagine Photography

ACKNOWLEDGMENTS

To my family and friends, who show me the meaning of love and perseverance every day.

To my ancestors, for making a way out of no way. Because of your example, I know what to do.

To my editors, Megan Joseph, Jessica Wick, and Clarence Young. Thanks for asking the hard questions.

To Jesse Hayes, for making ALL my stuff look good and believing.

To Karama, Shakima, and Dominique, thank you for taking my dream and making it bigger than I ever could have imagined. What can't we do?

And to Kisha, Nakeesha, Leslye, Lynn, Anika, Laurie, Sarah, Toya, Kenya, Noudjal, and Katia, for the constant encouragement and friendship.

To:

Breonna Taylor, George Floyd, Sandra Bland, Duante Wright, Rayshard Brooks, Daniel Prude, Atatiana Jefferson, Aura Rosser, Stephon Clark, Botham Jean, Philando Castile, Alton Sterling, Freddie Gray, Janisha Fonville, Eric Garner, Michelle Cusseaux, Akai Gurley, Gabrielle Nevarez, Tamir Rice, Michael Brown, Tanisha Anderson, Trevon Martin, and so many more.....

My heart is broken, but my will is strong.
I carry your heart, your potential,
every good thing you might have done – in me.
I will make something beautiful from it,
because you can no longer.

Watch over us as we carry on.

FOREWORD

Several of the stories in this collection came to me two years ago or more (I first dreamt the story for First Blood ten years ago!), but they all came to fruition between the latter part of 2019 and 2020 and that is significant.

2020 was a horrible year in many ways and there is no doubt that it ripened my pen for the stories in this collection. Almost all of them explore the violence of race in America in some way, shape, or form. It's not a subject I deal with usually in my fiction because, contrary to popular belief, I don't see tragedy and strife as the defining theme of African American people. I see us, our defining story, as one of spectacular triumph. I am the descendent of people who made the impossible happen. Not just once, but every day for about 500 years.

Black people in America have defied every obstacle put before them to have an influence that is palpable all around the world. The legacy of African American innovation in science, business, literature, visual arts, music, and culture is undeniable and there are only 42 million of us on the planet!

I am inspired by that legacy. I am honored to be counted among them – to add my small stone to the legacy of our collective excellence. To lift the next generation of Black creators higher, make it a little easier, as so many have done for me. I like to keep my art vibrating at that frequency because ours is not only a sad, mad, bad story. It's not even mostly a sad, mad, bad story. It's a story of possibilities and magic, hard work and fantastic vision. It's what I like to write about.

But in between my novels, my brain often turns to short stories as a way to reset my cognitive pallet while focusing on questions and thoughts that don't always make it into my books. Usually, I only write one short story, but one was apparently not enough for these times and so you have this collection.

I hope you enjoy reading it. But more than that, I hope you enjoy wrestling with the questions in these stories the way I did.

Happy Reading,
Cerece

FEAST OF THE FIFOLET

*M*allette rushed forward with the promise of blood so near she could taste it. The damp swell of night stretched across the shallow pools and marshlands of her home like a thick cloak, muting her sense of things near and far, yet Mallette had no trouble finding her way. Her slender wings slid through vines that tickled and scraped. Frightful creatures lurked by the riverbank, their eyes sliding back and forth with the surface of the water, but there was nothing more terrible than her tonight; no one else who dared hasten towards the echoes of agony that shook the forest.

The cries brought her to where the twisted limbs of the Mother Tree curled along the forest floor stretching nearly a hundred feet. Her bark was as velvety as the philodendron that peeks out from beneath the bush to catch the sun, with a canopy so wide it might one day shelter all the earth, given the chance. If Mallette had her way, the Mother Tree would live to see the next millennia and the one after that.

She slowed her pace and approached with reverence.

The hunter who was now her prey waited at the base of the tree, cursing and wailing in pain. Fear cut through his cries like a blunt ax as she drew near. His eyes squinted and bulged, desperate to make sense of the approaching bluish orb against the dark of the forest. Because he could not stand, Mallette kept herself low to the ground as she flitted about -- searching his face. His smell was familiar. She thought she knew him, yet with his features so contorted Mallette could not be sure.

His eyes crossed themselves as he struggled to track her movements. Beyond the terror and pain, she saw wonder. He had no idea who or what she was, and Mallette felt no compulsion to soothe his curiosity.

Instead, she darted away, past the open lacings of his trousers and the fresh smell of urine, to inspect the swollen flesh that bulged between the roots of the tree, where his foot lay twisted and crushed.

"Thank you, Mother!" she whispered. "Thank you for delivering our enemy to me."

The permission to do this, to reveal herself fully and set this plan in motion, had taken years to bring to fruition. In that time, many of her kindred had died eating the sorrow this hunter and those like him had wrought. After tonight, Mallette promised herself that —at least in her forest—there would be no more.

With shaking hands, he reached out to her. "Help me, please!"

The hard lines of his face flattened, and, for an instant, she could see him clearly. A familiar burning rose in her stomach. Mallette *did* know this man.

The tremor in his voice surprised her. An hour ago, the mob to which he belonged had been so boisterous they'd woken every sleeping animal in the forest and driven away those with the right to hunt by night. Mallette expected *some* crying. His foot was shattered. Still, she wouldn't have thought one so capable of cruelty could be broken so easily.

Perhaps he has no spirit at all, she mused. *Perhaps that is why he can cause so much pain yet endure so little.*

Given her own dilemma, she might have found some pity for the man, but the sour smell of alcohol drove her compassion to retreat—-that, and the charred body swinging just over his head.

Many men had come before these. Most did not have the wisdom to see the world beyond their own making, but those who did called her kind the Fifolet, spirits of the light.

Scared of what they did not know or could not control, the people told stories—wild stories of light-filled mermaids who lured men to the water's edge, only to feed them to their crocodile children. There were also myths conjured from their own minds about fairies who could transport mortals to a world of buried treasure, from which they would never return. Of course, none of these stories ever bordered truth, because those who fashioned them never ventured to learn or ask. They preferred their own legends to the reality of a story in which they had almost no part to play.

Born with the trees themselves, the Fifolet were brought into life by the Mother Tree to guard the sacred forests of the earth and care for the animal and plant life within. Spirits of the light existed long before Men came and, Life-willing, they would outlast them still.

Mallette drew closer and unfurled her wings just enough to hide her form yet keep her light and give her throat more air with which to form the words he would understand. Sweat drenched his face and his clothes held a foul stench Mallette felt sure would never dissipate.

"Please," he begged. "I can't move."

"Where are the others?" The words crackled painfully in her throat, though she'd practiced their strange-language many times.

"Please," he cried. "They left me here when the tree... attacked me."

Are there any tyrants who are not cowards? She wondered.

"You have to help me. I got a family."

Sparks of light burst from her wings before she could rein in her rage. She had eaten the refuse of his cruelty for years, yet now he sought mercy. She could not fathom the depths of his hypocrisy – a mirror of malice that never reflected back to its master.

Her eyes drifted upwards. "So did he," she replied. "A woman and two more, one still suckling the bitter taste of fear at his mother's breast. So afraid. They came running this way not two days ago. The crocodiles closed their mouths to let them pass. We drank his tears after he fell to his knees praying to his God and mine that his family would find safe passage. His name was Henry."

The man's eyes widened with new awareness. He

tried to pull away, but the Mother Tree's roots held firm. He whimpered where he lay.

"You don't know nothing about it," he cried, weak yet defiant. "Theys my property and if you know what's good for ya, you'll tell me where they went or you'll find the same kind of trouble Henry did. You got no right messin' with my livelihood."

"You are a strange breed, Aemon," Mallette replied. "In my world, to have something is to keep it safe from harm. Do you always destroy what is yours?"

"What?" Aemon stammered, straining to see through the light that dimmed as Mallette spread her wings. "How do you know my name?"

"Would that I didn't, that I'd never laid eyes on your face. But, no. You come here too often. We of the light all know your name. With our dying breaths, we have cursed you for poisoning our lands."

"What're you talking about? I never seen you before in my life!"

"Of course not! You lack the wisdom to see anything beyond your own world. Everything must be big, loud, and bright for you to take notice, but we know you. We have scraped the blood-boiled char off the trunks of our sacred trees with our teeth. Swallowed the bones and entrails of your victims as we tried to keep the poison sorrow from killing the ground beneath! For centuries, your kind have left us nothing but bitterness to swallow, until our bellies refused sustenance and our teeth rotted. Every time you came to this place, you did this.

"Before you, there were children and breadcrumbs, strawberry stumps and winterberries. The land was sweet and there was nothing to prune beyond the Shadow Moss and creeping vines that are too greedy for their own good. Until you. Now there are too few of us left to manage our own sacred duty. Rot and disease spread through the forest with not enough of us to stop it. Not enough to save each acorn, sapling, and root. All of this, because of men like you."

"There're trees everywhere! Christ! You can't walk two feet without seeing one."

"You think this now because you cannot see the future as I can. Because you do not know the consequences of what you do today."

Aemon's face crumpled with exhaustion. "I'm... I'm sorry. Okay? I don't know what you're talking about. I just need to get home. Help me?" The stillness of the forest was heavy as Aemon waited for his pleas to be answered. When Mallette did not move, Aemon's contrition quickly hardened into anger. Blue eyes blazed within a face that was tight and red with rage as he spat and bellowed. "My friends are coming back for me, you know. And when they do, they're gonna kill you and all your little fairy friends! We're gonna burn this goddamn forest to the ground! You hear me!"

Mallette's smile was small, sad, as a tear rolled down her cheek. This was the Aemon she had seen throughout the long years of change. She had not been wrong. This was the essence of the man she knew.

"Toby! Judge! Brett! Help!" he screamed.

Mallette snatched the sound from the air as he made it and held it in the palm of her hand. *They will come for you yet, Aemon, but only when we are done.*

Around them, the leaves of the Mother Tree glowed and quivered.

Aemon couldn't hear the voices echoing through the forest, but Mallette could.

"He wants to burn us," they hissed in their own sacred tongue. "Burn the forest as he does his own kind, the dark ones like us."

"He will kill us."

"He will kill us, but will we become killers, too?"

The children of light came slowly from the shadows.

Mallette's plan had not been popular. When the creatures of the forest refused to fill their bellies with the likes of him, she feared that she would need to eat him all by herself, a man nearly twenty times her size. But she would've done it. Unlike most of her surviving kindred, she had all her teeth. Her habit of cleaning them on the ivy that crawled along the forest floor kept them healthy and made them harder than they had been when she first came fully formed into being.

But now she knew she would not be alone.

Aemon still could not see her face. She was only light to him, a flame given human shape, hovering out of reach. But her true color was midnight: black hair, black eyes, black skin, blacker than any human could ever hope to be. Her wings carried her light. With them unfurled only moonlight could reveal her form, unless she chose to cast the infinite prism inside her out—-as she and the other Fifolet did for Aemon now.

The lights gathered as he scrambled to get away, to pull his foot free, but it was no use. Realization slowly transformed the fury on his face into understanding that no matter what he threatened, there would be no escape. Mallette's broad lips lifted again into the smallest, most terrifying smile.

Faces blacker than shadow emerged from within the dancing lights with large eyes wreathed in a celestial glow.

Her kindred whispered to him in the voices of children. "Will you kill us all?" they cried. "Burn the forest that feeds you?" Translucent lids fluttered and blinked.

Tears ran down his cheek. "No," he replied. "I swear. I only want to go home. Please, let me be."

Mallette said nothing as the Fifolet began to swarm. They could smell the truth for themselves.

"Lies!" one hissed.

Orbs of light circled around Aemon's head. Their words echoed in his ears like the buzzing of angry bees. "Many lies," they said. "He will be too bitter to eat."

"Yet, we must!" another answered. "To save what is left of the forest from sorrow."

Aemon hung his head in a fit of sobs. "But my family. They need me! They don't deserve this."

The Fifolet turned to Mallette.

"Who will we become if we do this?" they asked.

"Who are we if we do nothing?" she replied. "This man has brought this fate upon his family. Now he asks us to take on the burden he has treated so carelessly as our own. Should we think more of them than he does?"

"But they do not come to the clearing. They have not burned the bodies. Are they not innocent?"

"No more than we who witness and do nothing. Justice is useless to the dead. Nothing can bring them back. We can only keep the sorrow from spreading. His kin will carry his sorrow as we do."

"And save the Tree."

"And save the Tree."

"And save the Tree."

The light receded as the Fifolet unfolded their wings, leaving Aemon in darkness.

The first bite was sickening, a greasy mix of fear, shame, and ash, but then Mallette remembered the burned man's tears. The memory of his hope for his family and the knowledge that they would be safe eased the first chunk of flesh down her throat.

Beneath the sound of Aemon's screams, the animals of the forest were quiet and the Mother Tree twisted her great eyes away in sadness.

Taking no part in the matter, the crocodiles lined the riverbank in plain view at the men who hid at the forest's edge. This too was part of Mallette's plan. She knew Aemon's mob would return and when they did, faced with a power greater than their own, they would do nothing to help their friend. The animals of the forest watched the men run away with their torches unlit and their pick axes limp at their sides.

When it was over, the crocodiles would drag away whatever bones remained, while the Mother Tree hoped that the memory of the Feast of the Fifolet would ensure that no one would ever defile their forest again.

FIRST BLOOD

When I was born, my birth mother tried to kill me, to smother me at her own breast. Ma May says I fought and it was my cries that sent her and the other midwife to save me. Despite being born a slave, born a girl, born a Black child, I *wanted* to live. By the time they took me away, my mother had already left a scar, an ugly line down the length of my forearm. I thought she hated me until I came to understand that scar for what it was - my mother's first act of defiance.

To keep a child a child on a plantation is no small feat, but for most of my life I was one. Bereft of my mother's love, Mable—or Ma May as I call her—and the community of Black folk on the Lafayette plantation never left me wanting. I was doted on, protected, coddled and spoiled, as much as a half-breed child born of a slave mother gone mad could be, with the first pick of the Master's scraps from the table.

When I was old enough to help in the kitchen, Ma May would prop me up on two cushions and hand me vegetables to wash. Ma May was the head cook, and before she began work each day she would swing me 'round and 'round before plopping me dizzy and giggling on the big stool that only me and her son, Pepper, were allowed to sit on.

"You got that light shining in you, child," she would say, cutting up the remains of discarded apples into tiny bites so she could feed them to me one-by-one.

"Skin so light can't nothing keep it from coming through. That's what makes you so pretty."

Ma May would stroke my cheeks with her long, ebony fingers then turn back to the large cast-iron pot that was already simmering with the Master's lunch. Ma May's words made the apples sweet on my tongue and I beamed, proud that the most beautiful woman I ever saw thought that I was pretty, too.

"What's wrong with me? Why won't Mama look at me?"

"Nothing's wrong with you," Ma May replied. She held me firm by the shoulders and looked me in the eye.

"Then why?"

Ma May sighed, exasperated, tired. The first tear in the veil she'd tried to cast over the truth of my life already torn before there was anything she could do. I was six and Ma May took me to see my mama for my birthday, because I'd asked. I don't recall what I thought would happen, but it was nothing like I expected. She screamed and cried, recoiling at the very sight of me.

"It just hurts her still," Ma May explained. "Somebody hurt her real bad and that wound's never had the chance to heal."

"Did I hurt her?" I remember the sour taste of dread in my mouth as I waited for her reply.

"No, Noemie. You didn't do anything. It was your father. He touched your mama and she didn't want him to. You understand?"

At the time, I thought I did. It was one of the first lessons Ma May ever taught me. How to hit someone with a stick if they touched me in a way I didn't like.

"Beau said my daddy's White."

"He is."

"But I'm Black, like *you*." Something in my voice made Ma May smile.

"Yes, you are baby. You might look a little different from the rest of us, but underneath you just as Black as me."

She never took me back to see my mother again.

I spent most of my life in the kitchen under Ma May's watchful eye. From the chopping counter overlooking Ma May's garden, I came to know every face on the plantation and understand how life worked. With a staff of seven, including me, Ma May was in charge of feeding everyone. When my arms were strong enough to carry a steady tray, she would sometimes let me serve guests of the house drinks on the porch. But that was rare. Mostly, I chopped and washed dishes while Ma May taught me the magic of heat, butter, seasoning, and herbs. How to make a cut of beef sizzle in the pan yet melt in your mouth if the price of cotton was high, and how to make root vegetables from her garden into pies that tasted like meat if the price of cotton was low. Ma May kept me busy. If I wasn't slicing and dicing with growing precision everything that needed to be cut, I was gathering vegetables, fetching water, bringing crusts of bread to the fields for lunch when she could spare them, or delivering herb medicines, salves, and boiled bandages to those who were sick. They all smiled and took whatever help she offered through my hands, and in that way Ma May's goodwill passed on to me.

"Go on now," they urged kindly, patting my head through the wide straw bonnet that Ma May made me wear. "And keep that hat on before Master put you down here in the fields with us."

"I want to," I replied earnestly. "You get to be in the sun all day! Ma May almost never lets me outside."

They laughed until tears welled in their eyes then told me to hurry on. Only then did I head back to the kitchen, waving as Ma May watched me from the window. Even when I couldn't see her, I knew she was there. She never let me go anywhere she couldn't see me or stay in the big house past seven, no matter how much I begged her. Instead, she'd make Pepper walk me back to the cottage where we all slept together each night.

Everyone liked me. Everyone except Ma May's son, Emery, who most people called Pepper on account of the fact that he was as dark as the pots in Ma May's kitchen and everything else about him was hot and bitter to the taste. For Ma May, Pepper's smile was as bright as the full moon itself. His laugh flowed freely from someplace deep inside his chest. The sound always shook me when I heard it, like the rumble of distant thunder, yet his warm brown eyes were lit with mirth.

But that was only with Ma May. Everyone else got the silent treatment, which no one seemed to take to heart. I was the only one he treated with contempt.

It didn't help matters between us that he was the only one Ma May allowed to take food and supplies to my mother, the only other person on the plantation who hated me. He scowled as I skipped to the kitchen each morning. He rolled his eyes when I hummed in the garden. As a child, I used to think he was just another mean boy who enjoyed pulling my plaits, but as the years went by, I could not escape the fact that most boys were very nice to me, every boy in fact, except Pepper. Beau, the cobbler's son, was the nicest of all and had taken to bringing me flowers almost every day since the summer of my tenth year. Last week, I decided to give him a kiss on the cheek for his trouble, and he seemed to like it well enough. All Pepper and I did was fight.

"You don't know everything, Pepper!" I would often yell after one of our many arguments.

"Well, you don't know *anything*," he'd snap back, then walk away.

"Don't mind him," Ma May always soothed. "He just needs his daddy."

"What happened to him?" I asked, ploughing into her pain as only a thoughtless child could. Ma May's eyes filled with tears.

"Master sent him away," she sniffed, her face turned from me. "When Emery was just turning three years old." Between his height, which had always dwarfed mine, and the hard look in his eyes, I always forgot how close we were in age, nearly four years apart. My own father was a mystery to me. Ma May never mentioned him and so it was almost as if he didn't exist. But I'd never imagined the pain of having a real father and losing him. Pepper and I always seemed so far away from each other in everything. After Ma May's admission I finally began to understand why.

"Oooh, child! Ain't nothing like watching you with that knife in your hand!"

Proud to be the object of Ma May's praise, I diced the taters for the evening stew faster–showing off what I could do. She grinned and shook her head. I always felt better, more useful, with a knife in my hand.

"You remind me of stories my own mama used to tell about my granddaddy. He was born free in *Africa*. His people used to make patterns on their skin. He was *good* with them knives. He did it on himself, my grandmamma and my mother. She said it was to claim where we come from."

I frowned. "Wouldn't the cuts just scar?"

"It takes skill like my granddaddy had, like you got, and the right medicine for healing." Ma May reached out and tapped the tin of salve that she always kept above the stove.

"Like this. That's why all them kitchen burns and cuts we get heal up right. My mama taught me how to make it like her daddy taught her."

"Where are your marks, Ma May?"

I tried to choose my words with care. At almost thirteen, I knew better, but the sadness that was closer than I ever understood turned her voice down low.

"My mama was too afraid to give me any. The old master killed my granddaddy right in front of her for marking other slaves so they could find their families if they were sold away. After that, Master said we couldn't do it anymore."

Ma May was silent for a moment before turning to me with a tight smile. "But you. Even though you not my blood, you musta caught some of his spirit sure as I'm standing here."

"Maybe so." I shrugged, holding on to my knife handle and her words with an iron grip. "I just hope some of your magic rubs off on me."

"Magic? Girl, what you talking 'bout?" Ma May

poked the biscuit dough, testing its readiness before sliding it into the brick oven.

"Everything always seems to go your way. Your cooking. Your salves. All the medicines you make. Miss Llewellyn gives you the best clothes and everybody says you got the nicest cabin on the whole plantation. It's like things just work out for you is all." I scooped up the last of the potatoes and put them in the pot to boil. I looked up with a smile Ma May did not return.

"I ain't got no magic, Noemie. If I did, Miss Llewellyn woulda been dead long time ago. All I got is a deal with the devil herself, make no mistake. And Master ain't even a pinch better. Magic is a fairytale—something that's given, like fruit off the vine to pluck and use as you see fit. We Black. Nobody given us nothin'! What we got is *power*. You got to collect it grain by grain 'til it gathers and grows. You got to hold it in your hand and shape it from nothing into something. You got to earn it to wield it. No one can give it to you. You got to find it and make it your own, but once you have it and you *know* you have it, it's yours to keep. That's what I got. That's what we got. That's what *you* got." Her eyes flickered to the knife in my hand. "Shape yours into something you can use."

"Master's going to have my boy working *hard* today. Emery told me they got him breaking three new fillies from Louisiana."

"Well, I can take the food to Mama today if that'll help ease his back," I offered, trying to make my voice light while loading the trays to be taken into the dining room for breakfast.

There was a long pause before she spoke. "No. Emery'll do it. I already checked on your mother this morning. She not feelin' well. It's not a good time. Plus, I need you here cutting all them onions for the soup. You the only one who can cut onions all day and not shed a tear."

"Please, Ma May. I can help."

Ma May kept her eyes on her pots, but she didn't need to look at me to have my full attention.

"I said what I said. Now go tell Tess them trays ready to go out before the eggs get cold, then get back here. These onions ain't goin cut themselves."

With a sigh I knew well enough to hold inside, I turned towards the window. I was fourteen and while I loved Ma May as much as I ever had, the instinct for obedience felt harder and harder to come by. For the first time in my short life, the kitchen was not enough. I wanted more. I wanted answers.

The itch to test the boundaries of my life began two months earlier. Like almost any other day during the harvest season, I brought two pails down from the kitchen well to refresh the water barrel in the fields and doled out cups of water to all the workers because that day I could spare the time. It was so hot that when I looked up from scooping out a fresh serving, Pepper, who never came to me for anything, stood right in front of the line. Sweat flowed from the top of the jet-black curls on his head to the edges of his frayed pants right onto the dirt beneath his feet. He looked unhappy to see me as always, but, unlike every other day, when he drank his fill and handed the cup back to me, he spoke.

"You looking more like your mother."

At first, I couldn't say a word. By then I had no memory of her outside the twisted image of a woman screaming at me from when I was six. Even then, on the rare moments when I thought of it, the moment was shrouded in doubt and fear like a child's nightmare from long ago. I had nothing with which to replace it.

Pepper turned away.

"Like how?" I blurted.

It was then that I noticed the stillness around us. Every person within earshot of my question was frozen in place. Pepper looked up and scanned the cluster of people. There were warnings in their eyes, warnings I knew he could see–but his eyes settled back on me.

"I've only seen her once when I was small," I

explained. "I tried to go to her but she couldn't bear the sight of me. All she did was scream. I can't remember nothing about her but those screams."

Pain I didn't know I had burned through my insides. A tear ran down my cheek and for the first time in our lives together, Pepper looked at me with something other than a steady simmer of loathing. For the first time, when he met my gaze his eyes were filled with pity.

"Sundown. Behind the kitchen. I'll walk you home." I was stunned enough to think I misheard him, but not stupid enough to ask him twice. We were already risking the overseer's attention by talking this long. Pepper always walked me home. That wasn't anything new. But the promise of *more* in his voice was unmistakable. I would have to trust him and wait.

By the time Pepper showed up below the kitchen window with the heavy sun resting on his shoulder, I had so many thoughts they came spilling out the moment I hit the back porch.

"I want you to take me to her."

"I don't think she'd want to see you," he replied walking past me, but I caught up quick and stood in his way.

"Please."

"It would just upset her."

"She's my mother. I need to try to understand why she hates me."

"She doesn't hate you."

"You don't know that."

"No one hates you."

"You do." Just then, a thought occurred to me. "Why are you helping me, anyway?"

Pity rippled across Pepper's face again, but I didn't care. I'd take the path of pity if it led me to the truth.

"I don't hate you." Pepper's voice came soft. "I think your head's in the clouds half the time and you're spoiled, but I've never hated you."

"How am I spoiled?" It took gall for a house Negro to ask such a question, but I would not lay down my pride without a fight.

"People treat you different, better, on account of how you look. Sometimes, I think you like it that way." In Pepper's expression there was no malice. "Sometimes I think it makes you *think* you're better than the rest of us because of it. I can't fault you for it. We all want to be treated nice, but it's a lie. Master might use us different, but in the end, we all just slaves to him."

He'd walked us straight past our cabin to the creek. With all the washing from this morning long dried and hung, the water was almost still. But that was when it was most beautiful, with the last light of day breaking off the cliffs of each tiny rock and ripple. Pepper and I both liked to come here. It was, up until that moment, the only thing I knew for sure we had in common.

"You assume so much about me," I replied, staring out over the orange and red clouds. "I know I'm different, that I look different from the rest of you, but inside I *feel* the same. I am the same. You think I think I'm better than you but I know I'm not. It's you who can't see it, not me. How I look doesn't change who I am. I see you teaching yourself to read at night. You smart enough to know that."

Pepper responded with a deep satisfied hum before settling down by the water's edge.

"You know what happened to your mama, don't you?"

"Ma May told me that a White man touched her and she didn't want him to."

Pepper nodded. "After, Mama felt responsible, because Ma Clara took her shift that night. So she could spend some time with my Daddy before Master sold him to the Lees. When your Mama's mind never recovered, my mama made a deal with Miss Llewellyn so she wouldn't send her away. So she could look after you both."

"What deal?"

"I don't rightly know, but I think Mama makes a tea for Miss Llewellyn so she won't have no more babies by Master."

"How you know that?"

"Because Miss Llewellyn only asked for it after she spend the night with Master. Mama the only one who know how to make that tea so it work, but that's a bigger secret then me try'na read, so you best keep that to yourself, too."

I smiled at him, thrilled to have earned his trust, and, for the first time, Pepper smiled back.

After that, Pepper let me come with him sometimes to look in on Mama, or Ma Clara as he called her, but only if he felt she was strong enough. If she was, I usually stood outside her cabin, looking in but keeping my distance. Most days she couldn't meet my gaze, but it didn't hurt me so much now that I finally understood.

The day the pattern of my life finally fell together started like any other. Yet by midday Ma May sent me from the kitchen with a tight expression and instructions not to leave the cabin until she returned. Unaccustomed to idle time, I paced the length of the small room we shared, cleaning and worrying as I went.

I could feel her tension brewing the second her shadow fell in the doorway.

"Ma May, did I do something wrong?"

Ma May stepped fully inside, but didn't seem to see me. Instead, she went straight to emptying the contents of her basket on the bench by the door.

"Everything's happening too fast," she muttered. "Sooner than we planned, but nothin' to be done. We just got to see it through."

I stepped a little closer. "Ma May?"

"No, baby. You didn't do anything." Her weary gaze settled on me. "Your stomach still hurting you?"

I'd been so preoccupied with her being upset, that I'd all but forgotten about the nagging pull in my belly until she mentioned it. "A little."

Ma May nodded. I saw the spike of fear in her eyes, but I didn't know why and I was too afraid to ask.

"I brought you some tea and spirits. Take these," she said moving the bottles from her basket into view. "Sip them over the next few days when the pain hits you."

"I'm sure it'll be gone by morning. You don't send the others away when they sick. I'm not a child anymore."

"No. You're not," she sighed.

"I can work just as hard as they do. I promise. I'll be back in the kitchen by morning."

"No!" Ma May snapped, her far away fear coming into focus. "I have to go away. Master Lee's sick and they sent for me to go help him get better. I leave tonight. Until I get back you don't leave this cabin. You understand me? I made arrangements in the kitchen. You won't be needed and ain't no one going to ask for you neither."

Ma May placed a cup of medicine and my favorite kitchen knife by the wash basin.

"You stay right here 'til I get back. Only person you open that door for is Emery. He's gonna bring you food and water."

"Yes, Ma May. I understand." I didn't.

I watched Ma May pack. I remember how she looked at me, how she hugged me tight, then left without saying goodbye. I had no idea that she didn't have the heart to tell me that power, like innocence, is never given away. It is always taken.

I woke up the next morning with my first blood running down my legs. The red soaked through my clothes and the threadbare quilt that covered our thin mattress on the floor.

I hung the cleaned quilt out to dry and was just starting to scrub my nightdress when I saw Miss Llewellyn stumbling towards me like a ragged dog who'd been kicked around all night and come sniffing for a bone to soothe its pain.

"Where's Mabel?" she slurred without bothering to even look at me.

"She gone, Miss Llewellyn." I could see the tear

tracks all down her dirty face. "Master sent her to the Lee's."

She squinted, as if trying to recall a memory that refused to come. "Did she leave anything for me?" she asked finally.

"No ma'am."

She rubbed her face with both smooth pink hands. "Damn that girl! I need my medicine!"

She stood there looking wild, her breath coming out in ragged puffs of wine-soured air. But something in her settled as her focus finally rested on me. Her eyes made a jagged path between me, the nightgown, and the bloodstained water that swirled through my fingers.

"What you doing there, girl?"

I didn't know what to say. My actions were obvious. In my moment of hesitation, Miss Llewellyn closed in like a viper, grabbing me by the chin and holding my gaze. "When did your monthlies start?"

"Last night," I answered, confused by why she would be so interested.

"You're a woman now," she replied, releasing my chin and stepping back with a watery smile. The naked relief in Miss Llewellyn's eyes stunned me to tears. And all of a sudden, I did understand the reason Ma May wanted me hidden in our cabin, the reason behind every fence she'd tried to build between me and the

world she hoped I'd never know. I understood everything a moment too late.

"You come to the house as soon as your courses
finish. Ya here? You gonna stay with me now. I'mma fix
up a nice room for you and everything."

I knew they would have no effect, but the words
slipped out before I could stop myself. "Please, Miss
Llewellyn. Ma May told me not to leave the cabin."

"Did she now? I'm the Master's wife! You listen to
me! I expect you by the end of the week. Hear!"

I watched her leave, numbness and fear twisting
round in my belly, as I thought about how when she
arrived I almost felt sorry for her, but Ma May always
told me not to.

"She more evil than any person I ever met," Ma May
told me once when I caught Miss Llewellyn crying in
the drawing room one day. "Stay away from her. She'll
take her pain and choke you with it if you let her," she
explained, and Ma May don't lie.

It took me a few days, but I sought Beau first. With Ma
May gone and Pepper less talkative than usual, I
couldn't think of anyone else.

"I'm sorry, Noemie. Truly. Miss Llewellyn's as mean
as a kicked cat. She did the same thing to my sisters

before Master sold them away. They was pretty, too, but not like you. Your skin. All that fine hair. You special. You not like the rest of us."

I stepped back feeling sick, wishing he would stop talking.

"My mama told me before she died that this was bound to happen. She told me not to set my heart on you before the Master claimed you for his own, but I told her right then that I didn't care. And I still don't. I can share you, if I have to."

"Share me?" My voice came out in a whisper, though I was angrier and more hurt than I'd ever been in my life. He stepped forward as I moved further away.

"I don't want to, Noemie, but there's nothing I can do. You're so beautiful. I mean look at you." He reached toward my face. "You almost look just like 'em."

It was the worst thing he could have said. I didn't want to be beautiful. I wanted to be loved.

"Help me hide it. Help me, so only you can see!" I pulled the knife from my pocket. "Cut my hair. Cut me, so he can't see."

Beau recoiled. "I couldn't," he rasped.

I stopped crying. The tussle in my stomach, the ache in my head, everything stood still. When I spoke, my voice sounded like someone else's. "Not even to save me?"

"I love your face. How could I ruin it? You're asking

me to destroy what I love the most. You can't ask me to hurt you like that."

I turned and walked away.

When I reached Clara's cabin, I walked right in.

"Mama?"

She stirred on her cot, brown skin ashen from the creek where she'd tried to drown herself two nights before. Her body was frail with a pool of grief already brimming in her bloodshot eyes. I shuddered at the mirror of what I might become.

"I need your help."

Mama shook her head. "I tried," she wheezed. "But I failed. I don't know how."

"I know who my father is."

The last tear that hung in her eyes was fat with sorrow, but Clara wiped it away before it could fall.

"Who told you?"

"*She* did."

Understanding struck between us like lightning illuminating a common path that twisted and turned in an endless poison circle.

Clara sprang from her bed so fast I stumbled back, but my mother caught me with one callused hand on each shoulder. Her grip was painful, but I was numb to almost everything around me.

"She's sending you up to him."

Clara didn't ask. She knew. A deeper understanding of what my mother had been through clicked into place. "Yes. Tonight, after the evening meal."

"Where's Mabel?"

"At the Lee's. Master Lee fell sick. She's been gone four days now. I don't know what to do. Beau says he'll have me no matter what happens tonight, but he can't change the way things are. He said it was bound to happen on account of my face. He said there's nothing he can do."

"There ain't nothing he can do. What you need you have to find yourself."

I stared back at her, fighting against the grief of my own helplessness with no idea what she meant.

"When he took me," she rasped out, "I didn't know who I was. I just knew who I wanted to be. I thought I would be the type of girl who would fight. But I wasn't. When I saw that look in his eyes, like darkness with no end, I knew there was nothing inside me to match it. I was thirteen. I didn't know where true evil came from until then. For a long time there was just the nightmare of what he done and the heartbreak of what it brought me—a girl child—born to suffer her mother's fate."

"That's why you ran to the creek."

My mother nodded. "I've tried, Noemie. I wanted to be strong, but him, Miss Llewellyn, they broke me. I've never found enough pieces to put myself back together"

"But you *are* strong. You changed your mind. You came back."

"No. This is just the last time I tried to take my life. This time, Pepper pulled me out. Told me that you needed me and that I had to live long enough to help you."

My lips trembled as Clara released me from her grip.

"Do you hate me because I look like him?"

Clara's head jerked back. "Who told you that? You *my* daughter. No White man's blood can change that. You look like *me* and my mama, and her mother before her.

"I've loved you from the minute I found out I was carrying you. Mabel offered me her tea, but I couldn't take it. Then, when you were born, I was scared. So scared for you. I wished I'd had the courage to spare you this life, but I didn't. Everything you going through now is my fault. I'm sorry I brought such a beautiful gift into this ugly world. They don't deserve you."

Her eyes drifted down, from my forearm, where the scar she gave me still stood, to my hand and the knife within it. Her touch was as soft as her voice as she cradled my palm in hers and brought them closer.

"But maybe I was wrong. All this time I was afraid that you were like me, but you're not, are you? Maybe you know exactly who you are."

I looked at my mother, clear eyes meeting a wistful smile.

"Finish what I started," she said, tracing the scar with her fingertips. "All those angry, hard bits. All the hurt parts that linger so deep. We need to cut 'em loose. Let your insides out, Noemie. Our real beauty should only ever be seen by those who love us."

I returned to Ma May's cabin and took my time cleaning the place that had been my home. I swept the floors and shook out the rough curtains with care. Saying goodbye to the life I knew with my mother's words ringing in my ears.

Pepper barged in just as I was mending the edge of our newly washed quilt, bringing the smell of forest and soot with him.

"Where you been! I looked all over this plantation for you! Mama told you to stay here! I been worried sick!"

Pepper had barely ever shown enough emotion

toward me to raise his voice, much less worry. But the sight of him rushing forward to wrap me in his arms sent a wave of relief through me I didn't know I'd waited all my life to feel. Though I knew it couldn't last, I brought my arms around his back to return the first physical contact we'd ever had.

"Mama told me to look after you. You not safe without her here. Master's been abusing Miss Llewellyn all week. No telling what that woman's fittin' to do."

I know.

"I'm sorry I worried you." My voice was muffled against the warmth of his chest, but I would not move. "You have enough to deal with." Pepper drew back, looked at me, and frowned. I knew then that he'd heard something in the thin tenor of my voice, but he couldn't place its meaning, not with so much else going on.

"We all do," he replied, holding my gaze. "Tonight, we leave this place. Mama set it up with my Daddy at the Lee plantation. You stay here 'til I come and get you. Sometime after Master goes up from supper. We burnin' the crops, then we runnin'."

I smiled. He wasn't asking me. He was trusting me and making sure I understood the plan.

"Tonight, we gonna be dead or we gonna be free, one way or another."

Tears of joy for him and the community of people I loved filled my eyes. We had the exact same plan. Pepper just didn't know it.

But my silence didn't sit well with him. "You with me, right?"

My smile was slow as the rising sun, but I could feel the power of it in the shine it made across his face.

"We gonna be dead or we gonna be free," I repeated. "One way or another."

He heard it again, something missing that threatened to pull him into the no-win situation I had chosen. He wanted to follow me there for reasons I was only starting to guess, but I couldn't let him. I would not let him.

"Noemie?"

I placed both hands on his cheeks and held his gaze, grateful for the fact that he knew me, understood me, much more than I ever realized.

"I'm with you, Emery. All the way."

I marveled at my reflection. I had only stepped into the finely appointed bedroom Miss Llewellyn gave me a few hours ago, yet everything around me was altered by the design of my own hands. In the background, I saw the yellow satin dress that Miss Llewellyn laid out

for me still on the bed, stained but intact. In my fore-
ground, the woman I was stood tall. Without the length
of hair to weigh it down, my curls sprang free and wild
about my head in three inch coils of sable and gold.
The dark red marks that ran across my forehead and
cheeks were almost dry. Finishing what Ma May's
granddaddy and my mama began, I staked claim to the
land of my people and cut the wounds deep enough to
set my soul free.

Some called it blood, but I knew better. The thick
liquid scalded my skin, leaving ribbons as red as rage.
Outside, Pepper lurked, preparing to set fire to the first
of the Master's crops. I smiled. The wounds that would
cut scars across my dimples for life ached. But birth *is*
painful. It costs to create, always.

Growing up on a plantation, I'd seen the face of
cruelty many times. Yet I'd never known its darkness,
been the object of its desire until that day. In my igno-
rance, I'd never considered how fine a thing pure
violence, born of righteousness, could be until I bathed
in my own father's blood.

I waited for him by the nightstand; naked as the day
I was born, as naked as he wanted me to be. With my
face already marked but my hair yet to be shorn, I kept
my head down, luring him in, inviting him to touch.

"They say you're one of mine. God forgive me if it's
true," he rasped, leaving the door slightly ajar. I turned

around when he told me to and stuck my knife in his gut like a period at the end of a long ugly sentence. It was the last time I would ever do what I was told again.

Piece by piece, I carved his cruelty into a beautiful tapestry of blood and entrails that covered the walls, stained the bedding, and soaked the rug. I made the wounds on his body as brutal as his intentions. Unlike the cuts I left on him, mine would heal into the pattern I'd chosen. I would be as beautiful as I'd ever been, but now only those who truly loved me would see it best. His wounds would fester and rot long after his death at my hands.

Miss Llewellyn's reflection in the mirror ruined my revelry.

"You... You killed him!"

Like two predators, our eyes locked on each other, then searched for the nearest weapon. I was slightly farther away from the knife, but she was also faster than I thought. I should not have been surprised. Miss Llewellyn had murdered spirits, minds, souls, many times over. She was used to stepping on and over the dead. My father was my first kill.

She wrested the knife from his chest with ease, as though she'd done the deed herself, then turned eyes that were full of death on me. I saw the darkness and stumbled. My spirit was ready, but *my mind* was still unprepared. I reached for her right hand, trying to take the knife away, but in my singular focus, I did not see her left arm swing round with a punch that sent me crashing down. By the time I hit the floor she was on top of me, aim pulled back and ready to stop my heart just as it had learned its own rhythm. In a flash I thought of Emery, Ma May, Clara, and all the people I cared about that I would never see again.

I did not have one regret.

I swung out wildly, clawing at her arms and face, determined not to *give* her my life. But at the moment her arm plunged down, her head snapped back, causing her aim to miss. The knife fell from her hand as one ashen brown arm coiled around her neck, pulling her away from me.

Clara.

Miss Llewellyn kicked and scratched as they whirled around the room, crashing into everything, growling at each other, but my mother never lost her grip.

"Mama!" I screamed as Miss Llewellyn used her body to thrust Clara into a wall with so much force I could hear my mother's jaw snap shut. Sweat poured down her face and her arms were bloody and trembling with the effort it took to vanquish so much hate, but when Clara looked at me, for the first time, her eyes were clear.

"Go!" Her voice was calm as the woman within her grip thrashed and foamed at the mouth.

Clara's eyes shifted to the window and the burning fields below. She did not spare another glance my way, as she cocked one leg against the wall, then pushed, propelling herself and Miss Llewellyn through the window and down into the vast silence that final freedom brings.

I would not waste the gift she gave me. Shaken, I put back on the only clothes I had, grabbed my knife off the floor, slathered Ma May's salve on my face, then headed out only to find Pepper flying up the stairs with a machete in one hand and a rifle in the other.

"You supposed to be gone!" I cried, both relieved and worried to see him.

"Beau told me where you were. I came to get you." His eyes scanned my body, not my face, searching for any sign that I was harmed.

"He didn't touch me."

Pepper nodded. "I saw Ma Clara and Miss Llewellyn. She…"

His eyes shone with grief, but I took his arm and held it tight.

"She bought me my freedom."

Behind Pepper, the plantation was ablaze.

"Freedom suits you," Pepper said, placing a gentle hand on my shorn head.

I moved down the stairs. "Then let's go."

When we got outside, every slave I knew was in a state of flight, except Beau, who stood by the water barrel with a black eye and a busted lip, trying to convince people to stay and fight the fire. I didn't have to wonder who had given Beau his bruises. His eyes fell on me briefly with a look of horror before Pepper and I joined the current of Black people running.

"What about Ma May?" I asked, panting to keep up as we ran toward the forest.

"If they made it out, she and my daddy gonna meet us farther down the creek."

"Then what?"

"We take our freedom, any way we can."

I smiled as he locked his hand in mine, our feet finding a new rhythm as we ran toward the future and never looked back.

BLUE HONEY

"*C*ome on down, Tut. Breakfast is ready!"

Charles IV, or Tut as he was often called, rolled out of bed not quite ready to face the day. The headache that greeted him every morning pounded against his skull as if it were a prisoner trying to break free. His bones ached and his stomach churned with a queasiness that food would not settle. But that was not the worst of it. The weight of the week was heavy in his father's voice. The fatigue. The despair. The emptiness.

"Okay, Dad. I'll be right down."

Even the sound of his own voice hurt. Tut felt sure he was older than his father in every respect except affairs of the heart. On that account, Tut was glad to have youth on his side. At only twelve years old, he was too young to have a girlfriend, much less a broken heart.

"I made Mom's pancakes!" his father added.

Of course you did, Tut thought. *It's Friday.*

It was their tradition. His mom's pancakes and a story to keep her alive, to memorialize her passing three years ago, and to see a wisp of his father's smile. Sometimes Tut wondered how his father would remember him after he was gone.

Tut made an effort not to hobble as he walked down the stairs.

"All right! Come on before everything gets cold."

Tut tried to hurry, then thought better of it when his left knee seized. He suppressed his groan but it was too late. By the time he was at the bottom step, Charles III was already there.

"Sorry, son. How are you feeling?" His father leaned in, ready to support Tut's weight and lift him up if necessary, but Tut waved him off, annoyed by the truth that he was still small enough that his father could carry him like a child.

"Don't worry. I just took a wrong step. Breakfast smells good."

"Well, you know. Your mother knew how to cook."

"You can, too." Tut's eyes washed over the spread. Pancakes, eggs, bacon, sliced tomatoes with avocado and onion, fresh rolls, and tea with milk. Everything was organic and locally sourced, a remnant from his mother's dogged attempts to combat the toxicity she'd been exposed to as a child from the chemicals used in oil drilling around her house. Tut didn't know why they still bothered. She'd died of the same cancer that was killing him. Beside the organic feast were all his pills, lined up and waiting.

Charles—Professor Tillman to his colleagues— watched Tut settle into his chair at the kitchen table before he continued. "Aah. I mostly do what she tells me. I can still hear her voice in my head telling me, 'Those greens don't have no taste.'"

Tut smiled. Charles did not, but Tut knew how to fix that.

"So, you have a story for me?"

For the next thirty minutes, his father came alive. It was Tut's turn to cry with laughter or grief, chasing the bitter knowledge that became clear every Friday that he hadn't just lost his mother three years ago. When she died, she took his father, too.

After taking in the small portion of breakfast that he could stomach, Tut choked down the cocktail of vitamins that was supposed to make his chemo treatments tolerable. A few feet away, his father made stacks of the dishes that would serve as his late-night distraction. When Charles was done, he would put on his hard hat with the blue light, snap on a long range walkie-talkie and a baby monitor to either side of his belt, and go down to the cellar, into what Tut had come to see as the mouth of his father's madness.

He had stopped asking to join his father six months ago, but by then Charles' research into the life of an extinct species of bee had turned from a professional fascination to a singular fixation with one goal: to find a cure for Tut's cancer.

When his mother, Helena Graves Tillman, was first diagnosed, Tut remembered his father's faith in the medicine the doctors prescribed. Helena had always been the picture of vibrancy and everyone *knew* she would live. She walked out of her last chemo treatment with a full head of untamable curls, her family at her side and her whole life ahead of her. They moved to Sasabe, Arizona to follow his father's research as an entomologist on a little known and extinct ancestor of the Exaerete Smaragdina, or Orchid bee. Within a year, Helena was dead. A month later, her son was headed down the same path.

Around the same time, Charles made a curious discovery in an underground cave a few miles from their house—the remains of a Native American man killed by a bullet to the heart. Charles found the man perfectly preserved, with an ovipositor in his forearm and traces of a blue substance in his stomach. His colleagues at Cornell University didn't think much of it, assuming his condition was due to the location of his death or ingesting some type of preservative poison from a long extinct plant. They dismissed the presence of honey in his stomach, assuming its strange aqua-blue appearance was due to some corrupting chemical, but Charles saw something else. An idea coiled around the loss of his wife and the fresh grief of his son's diagnosis, binding them together into a solution only he could see: The existence of a species of bee that was not extinct, but merely hidden underground. A species whose honey could stop the deterioration of cells for over 400 years. A honey that had evolved so thoroughly that it was blue.

Charles began digging beneath their house that night and, for the past three years, he dedicated himself to the discovery of blue honey. In between home-schooling his son and hiring a nurse to administer Tut's treatment, Charles dug.

He was convinced that the honey these bees produced could preserve tissue, as it did in the case of the Native American man. If their larvae consumed the honey, it stood to reason that their descendants should be alive somewhere.

At first, Tut would dig with his father out of

boredom and the simple desire not to be stuck sick in the bed all day. But as the months turned to years, Tut grew weary of dark tunnels and his father's growing need for isolation. Charles stopped consulting with his colleagues and friends. No one came to visit them anymore except the contractors who Charles hired to dig. For Tut, it seemed the larger the tunnel grew, the more it buried them alive.

Charles dug almost every day.

Sometimes he slept amidst the dirt, mumbling to himself about the bees. Tut found him there one night, after a nightmare caused him to leave his bed and seek out his father.

"Dad?" Tut had called into the cavernous space. Even with decent lighting and the trolley Charles built to travel through the tunnel, it took several minutes to find his father. When he did, Tut wished he'd stayed in bed. Charles was passed out on the floor with the blinking baby monitor strapped to his belt. Jars of urine and excrement lined the edges of the tunnel, while discarded scraps of foil littered the ground, barely containing the smell of their half-eaten remains. Tut exited the trolley more frayed than he had ever been before, and curled up next to the only parent he had, a man too tired to hear his own son's voice, and cried. He never went down to the cellar again.

Three years after Charles's discover, the tunnel

beneath their house and the distance between who they were and who they had been as a family spanned more than a dozen miles, bracketed and framed, but still in danger of collapse.

"It's been a while since you've been in the tunnel. I'm making real progress. You should come see." The anticipation in Charles' voice broke Tut's heart, but he knew he couldn't do it. One of them had to remain sane.

"I've still got that calculus homework you gave me to finish." Tut chewed the inside of his lip for a bit. "I might need some help."

His father shook his head. "Don't worry. You'll get it. You got your mother's mind. You'll figure it out. If you get into trouble, you can reach me on the walkie. I'll talk you through it. You'll need all of that math when I find that honey. You're gonna pull through this, Tut. You'll see."

"Dad."

"I know it's taken some time, but I'm close."

"Dad."

"Just last week, I was looking at the tissue samples from the subject I found in the cave. His cells are still as healthy as the day he died. If that honey can keep them from atrophy for 400 years, just imagine what they can do for you."

Tut stared at his father, watching him shuffle around, piling dishes neatly in a kitchen that was falling apart. Ignoring the signs, ignoring his son. The morning dew of Tut's sadness evaporated into anger.

"Dad!"

They didn't raise their voices in the Tillman house unless it was in laughter, but joy had left their home years ago. Charles startled, breaking a plate against the edge of the porcelain sink and cutting his finger. At first, neither of them noticed.

"I'm dying!" Tut yelled to his father's back, more furious that he had to spell it out than the fact that it was true. "The treatments aren't working, just like they didn't with Mom. I'm gonna be dead in a few months, while you're down there in that tunnel looking for some bees that left here a million years ago. I'll be dead and you probably won't even find me for a week!"

Charles' body swayed slightly with exhaustion, with pain, with fear. He watched his blood swirl down the dirty dishwater and find its way to the drain. *How much would I give to see my son live*, he thought. *Every last drop.*

He turned toward Tut and allowed himself to see with his heart what his eyes had been cataloging for weeks—the gray cast over his son's honey-brown complexion, the ten pounds he'd lost in just the past week, the dark circles under young eyes, eyes that flashed open in pain and held it in rather than crying out, so as not to worry a father who heard it all anyway.

No. The medicine wasn't working, but that was no surprise. Charles watched it fail his wife. Why would it work now?

I need to find that honey.

"Dad, you're bleeding!" All the anger in Tut's voice was gone, replaced by a heavy layer of regret.

Charles grabbed the nearest kitchen towel and wrapped his finger. He saw the tears in his son's eyes, tears he knew all about, but Charles couldn't join him in shedding them.

Tut's right, he thought. *We don't have much time.*

"You're not going to die," Charles began. "I told you. I'm close. When I find the honey, you're going to get better. You've got to trust me, Tut."

But Tut didn't trust him. Not anymore.

"Dad, please. You need to rest."

Tut was ashamed. As he looked at his father, he realized Charles was not the only one guilty of neglect. The man before him seemed at least five years older than he'd been a month ago. His face covered in a wiry gray beard that spanned the full length of his cheeks and neck. To be honest, Tut couldn't remember the last time he'd seen his father's clean shaven face. Charles' clothes drooped with a fine layer of dust that seemed to have become a part of the fabric itself.

All this time, Tut had told himself his father was lost to the grief of losing his wife and, soon, his son, but now he knew what a childish interpretation that was. His father was not lost, he was broken. Looking into Charles' weary eyes—eyes that had not had one second more of rest than his body insisted—Tut understood that it was not just him who was dying. When he died, his father would not survive.

"I'm fine," Charles replied, inspecting the clotting of his finger. "You're the one who needs to rest. You can work on the calculus tomorrow if you're too tired."

Tut watched his father power up the baby monitor at his waist, grab his hard hat, and open the cellar door.

"Dad, you can't keep doing this."

"Your mother used to pray. If you're worried, you should try that," Charles offered.

Tut frowned. "You're a scientist. I thought you didn't believe in God."

"Of course, I do," Charles replied. "I married your mother."

Tut waited until his father closed the door behind him, then listened for the fading sound of footsteps and the slow creek of the tunnel trolley carrying him away before moving towards the phone in the living room.

His father needed help and Tut couldn't wait any longer to seek it out.

"I'm so glad you called, Tut. You shouldn't have had to deal with this all on your own." Marrell sighed into the phone. "I thought he'd let that bee thing go years ago."

"How come you never called?"

"I'm your godfather, Tut. Of course I called. We all did. But your Dad never called back. We just assumed he needed more time to grieve and take care of you. I had no idea he hadn't talked to Aunt Jay in over a year. I'm sorry. Really I am."

Tut wiped his tears and listened.

"Look," Marrell continued. "The University's had Charles on sabbatical for awhile now. Everyone misses him. He just needs help." Marrell laughed nervously. "It's not like things are busy. Not like when your father was here. Charles was always the innovator, you know. —without him, both the money and the projects have dried up. But don't worry. You did the right thing. A few of us will be down by Monday."

"He's not going to want to leave, Uncle Mar. He swears something's down there."

"Don't worry about that, Tut. We just need to get the right people to help him."

Suddenly, Tut had a flash of orderlies hauling his father away in a straightjacket.

"Okay, but they're not going to hurt him, right? I just think he needs to rest and maybe someone to talk to. I don't want him to be alone if I die." Tut was trying to sound hopeful and mature, like the grown-up he wasn't, but needed to be right now.

"Of course not. Your father and I grew up together. I'm gonna call your aunt when we get off the phone. We'll figure out a place for you to stay while your dad gets better. You just take care of yourself. We'll see you soon."

Tut had expected to feel better after sharing the secret he'd carried for so long. Instead he felt exhausted and slightly soiled from the act of betraying his father's trust.

Why had his father not told his colleagues about his work? Tut wondered. He couldn't fathom the reason yet his stomach turned in knots. Tut went upstairs and fell into a restless sleep worried about how his father would react when he found out what Tut had done.

"Tut! Wake up, son. I found it!"

As usual, Tut couldn't tell if it'd been five minutes or

eight hours since he fell asleep. The medicine was like a weighted blanket over his bones.

"Dad?"

"Come here." Charles lifted Tut from the bed and carried him down the steps.

"I don't feel good," Tut muttered, still half asleep against his father's chest. "The medicine's stuck in my stomach."

"Don't worry about that. I found some new medicine for you. Just rest. I'll take you to it."

Tut lifted his head trying to focus. "What do you mean?"

Charles lowered his son into the trolley, then squeezed into the small bench beside him. "You'll see soon enough."

Tut woke to the sound of soft buzzing. Though his back was against a jagged, rough surface, he was covered in a warm blanket. The air was moist and his lips were coated with something sticky. His tongue tingled with the taste of honey.

He opened his eyes to a luminous blue-green world and the dancing glow of thousands of round, iridescent blue bees.

"Shhh. Don't speak. Take this," Charles said.

Before he could utter a word, Charles angled a spoonful of honey into Tut's mouth. His eyes went wide. The taste was both sweet and tangy, like honey and lemon mixed together. It also had a slightly grainy texture he did not expect. It went down easier than anything Tut had consumed in the last two years. He touched his fingers to his lips.

"Dad, it's blue! What is this?" A large bee landed on Tut's nose for a second, startling him upright. His movement was almost fluid, without pain.

"Don't worry about them," his father said with a chuckle. "As far as I can tell the worker bees don't sting. And so what if the honey's blue? Can't be worse than the poison you've been taking for years now."

Tut's eyes widened as he turned to Charles and watched the utterly unfamiliar sight of his father's smile, broad and full enough to show off both rows of bright white teeth.

"You found them," Tut whispered.

"I told you I would."

Tut looked around, stunned by everything he was seeing. Over the years, his father had shared his theories on what an underground hive of ancient bees might look like. Charles had described it so thoroughly – from the need to develop bioluminescence to the round shape of the bees and the size of the massive honeycombs that spanned the length of the tunnel in every direction – that the sight before Tut felt like waking up from a vivid dream, only to find it was real.

His father wasn't crazy. He was a *genius.*

"It's just like you said it would be."

His father chuckled again. "It's more than that," Charles replied, an air of seriousness cracking through his joy. "Have some more, then get some rest. When you wake up, I'll show you around."

"What about you?" Tut asked, wondering if his father had taken any of the honey for himself.

"I already stuffed my belly *full.* After all these years of digging, I was hungry!"

Tut closed his eyes and smiled. His father had just made a joke.

For the first time in so long he couldn't remember, Tut woke up to silence. The painful throbbing that accompanied him every morning was gone. He rose from the floor on legs that were light, spry—finally in the body of a twelve-year-old boy once more. His stomach growled wanting food.

"Dad! It doesn't hurt!"

Charles began to run, his voice carrying back from far down a glowing blue tunnel. "What hurts? Tut? Don't worry, I'm coming now."

"*Nothing* hurts!" Tut shouted back, laughing as he jumped back and forth on nimble feet.

"Already? You sure? You just spent two days sleeping on the ground."

Tut could hear the relief, the presence of lightness in his father's slightly labored voice. The echo of his footsteps running made Tut smile.

Two days, Tut shrugged. *No wonder I feel so good.*

"Dad, where are you?"

"Down a ways. I didn't expect you to wake up so soon."

"Stay there. I'll come to you."

Charles' stopped, a twinkling smile spreading on his face. "You sure you can make it? It's a good ten-minute walk."

"Yeah, Dad. I'm sure. I feel good. You got any food down here?"

Charles held his hand over his mouth to suppress a sudden sob and leaned back against the wall. *There's my boy*, he thought. It had been so long since he'd heard Tut express a hunger for anything.

"Dad?"

Charles cleared his throat. "Yeah, there's a jar of honey and some water to the right. Eat it slowly."

Tut leaned over and guzzled down the first canteen of water within reach before grabbing a mason jar of honey. "Okay, tell me where to go."

"Just keep walking towards the sound of my voice."

Though the hum of the bees was always there, their numbers had dissipated quite a bit since Charles first discovered them, shifting the sound in the tunnel from an anxious buzz to a low, steady hum. As Charles listened to his son's footsteps start, then pause, he wished he could see Tut's expression. Impatient, he began walking, picking up his pace.

Conversely, Tut hadn't moved more than a few feet from where he first woke up. Candescent aquamarine honeycombs surrounded him, replacing what should have been dirt walls with massive hexagonal structures or varying sizes, stacked upon each other from ground to ceiling. Each facet was sealed with a hardened substance that reminded Tut of resin, except for the blue color. Fascinated, Tut gulped down honey and stepped closer. Beyond the translucent surface of the combs, he saw what looked like a bird, though it's long beak and wings were unlike any bird Tut had ever seen. His gaze travelled from one comb to another, finding another bird, what looked like a metallic rock, then, in another comb, a tiny insect.

"Dad! What is all this? Why are there *things* trapped in the honey?"

"I'm not sure exactly, but I think these bees use the preservative qualities of their honey to do more than just feed their larvae and prolong their own lives. I think these bees store history, the Earth's history."

"Like archaeologists?" Tut asked, pushing his words through another mouthful of honey.

"Or librarians. I'm not sure which yet. So far, I've only explored about five miles of the tunnel and I found stores of plants that have been extinct for millions of years and small insects, but I suspect this nest goes on for quite a bit longer."

"Aah!" Tut shrieked. "They got spiders in here! Big spiders!" Through the blue glow of the honey, the spider's frozen yellow eyes looked green and menacing.

"They *have* spiders here," Charles corrected as he placed a steady hand on Tut's shoulder. "And there's no need to be afraid. Everything here, except the bees and us, is dead. Nothing can harm you." Charles appraised his son, cataloguing the color of his skin, the clarity in his eyes, and his unburdened stance.

"Did you find any… humans?"

Charles smiled. "I found a few specimens, yes."

Tut's mouth hung open. "For real?" He stuffed another spoonful of honey in his mouth. Charles noted that the jar was almost empty. *So much for eating slowly.*

"Did you drink any of the water I left?"

"Yeah, I finished that first."

"Let's sit down. I want to take your vitals."

As Charles expected, Tut had a lot of questions.

"So, what if these bees are like killer bees? What if they killed those humans and ate them?"

Charles looked up from the gauge he was monitoring. "I'm glad to see your imagination is in as good a shape as your blood pressure. You need to stop watching all those low-budget horror movies. Only a few prehistoric bees were carnivorous."

Tut raised his eyebrows unconvinced.

Charles smiled. "The human specimens I found were intact. No signs of mass bee feedings."

"You talk about my imagination," Tut replied incredulously. "What about all this? You imagined all of this before you even found it!"

"I see your point," Charles conceded. "But... This isn't what you think."

"What do you mean?"

"I can't be sure at what point in the hive we are, but the objects I've observed started out with just bees. Bees don't typically hunt their own species, so I couldn't figure out why these bees would store them until I realized that the bees preserved within the honey were the exact species or predecessors to the species in this cave. It stands to reason that within a species of bees that can sustain themselves over a long period of time, death would be a rare occurrence. When one of their own died, I think it would be a mystery of sorts, something they might want to try to understand so they could find a way to adapt.

"I found dinosaur eggs stored with the same prehistoric samples. I also observed what I think is hardened lava, then later humans. Of course, I wouldn't dare disturb the structure of their honeycombs to extract anything, but in one place, I saw a branch covered with ash. I even found an entire car."

"How would a bunch of bees lift a car?"

"Its placement suggests that the bigger items settle down here from above."

"But why? Why would bees save a car?"

"I think they are historians, like you said. They are charting the history of their species and perhaps more specifically the threats to their species, and in doing so, they have also preserved the history of the world."

Tut leaned forward. "So after they solve the mystery, you think they're gonna, like, rise up and attack us?"

Watching his father roll his eyes made saying the foolhardy idea worth it.

"Hold this under your tongue and use the time to think," Charles teased, shoving a thermometer in Tut's mouth. "We like to think that things like killer bees are the greatest threats to the world, but that's never been true. Outside of the occasional meteor, *we* are the biggest threat to our existence. Look at you and your mom. The odds of you both getting the exact same type of rare cancer in nature are too small to bother calculating, but you did. The reason for that is likely exposure to something man-made, something that killed your mother and almost killed you.

"Historians don't study history to change it. They study history to understand it and perhaps predict or change what might happen next. Bees are intelligent creatures. They communicate, problem-solve, and make decisions. I think they're trying to solve a puzzle. And this species of bees has adapted to continue their work over hundreds of thousands of years."

Charles slid the thermometer from Tut's mouth. "Ninety-eight-point-six. Your vitals are strong. Stronger than I've seen them in a long time. How do you feel?"

Tut shook his head. "Dad, I'm sorry I doubted you. I wish. I wish Mom..."

"Me, too," Charles said. "But if I hadn't lost her, I don't know if I would've been as determined to find this hive and save you."

"Man, I can't wait till Uncle Mar gets here and finds out what you did! They're not gonna believe it."

Charles froze. "You invited him here?"

Tut swallowed, his stomach turning in familiar knots.

"Yeah, I told him I was worried about you. He said him and Aunt Jay would come visit to see if they could help."

Charles' eyes darted to the tunnel and back to Tut. "When? When did you tell him?"

"Just before I came down here. Yesterday."

"Tut you've been asleep for two days! How long did he say it would take him to get here?" Charles grabbed his son by the shoulders. "Think, Tut. I need you to be sure."

"Dad, I'm sorry. I thought you were going crazy. He did, too, but now everybody's gonna know."

"Tut, listen to me. No one can know about this. No one."

Shock and confusion rippled through him. "Why?"

"It's taken these bees millions of years to preserve their history, the history of the entire world maybe, but it will only take a few minutes for humans to destroy. We can't let that happen."

Suddenly, their whole life over the past three years clicked into place.

Tut stepped out of his father's grasp. "That's why you stopped letting people visit us."

"Yes. Once I theorized that the preservative proper-ties of their honey would most likely extend to the bees themselves, I knew I didn't want to involve other people before I understood the full extent of the implications. I expected something extraordinary, but I never imagined anything like this."

"Uncle Mar said he's bringing some people from the university, too. He said they'd be here in three days."

Charles gasped. "That's today!"

"I'm sorry, Dad. I didn't think—" but Charles cut him off.

"No, Tut. This is my fault. I asked you to trust me, but I never told you why. It'll be okay, I have a plan, but you need to leave here. Go live with Aunt Jay for a while. Just until you turn eighteen, then you can come back here if you want to."

"And what are you gonna do?"

"I have to stay. Seal the entrance and protect the hive."

Tut shook his head. "I'm not leaving you."

"Tut, you're just getting better. You have so much you need to see and do. You can't live the next six years of your life in this tunnel with me."

"What if the cancer comes back and I can't get to you?"

"Tut, their honey preserved a dead man, keeping his cells from deteriorating. *Healing* them so that they would not decay. I don't know how long you'll live, but

I'm almost certain your cancer is gone. You can have a full life. Maybe many lives."

"Then I want to spend one of them with you. Who says you're the only one who knows about this? There could be a million access points to this hive."

"Maybe, but *this* is the one that *I* know about, so this is the one I have to protect. This is my burden, not yours."

"I wish you'd stop thinking like that. We're supposed to be a family. It's just you and me now."

Charles reached out and held his son tightly in his arms. "I don't want you to leave," he whispered fiercely. "I just got you back."

"You're my father," Tut cried. "I want to stay with you. Maybe Uncle Mar will agree with you. Maybe he'll keep it a secret, too." But even as Tut said the words he doubted them.

"He won't, Tut. There was a time that I would have believed he was that kind of man, but he's not."

Tut thought about the anxious hitch in his godfather's voice when he talked about needing Charles back. The department's need for funding. No, they would not respect his father's wishes. They would exploit every discovery, every bee in this hive, until it was gone. Still, Tut wasn't sure.

"What about the honey? If it cured me, imagine how

many other people it could save? We would be selfish to keep it, knowing that, wouldn't we?"

"I have been selfish. When I first started looking for the honey, all I thought about was a cure for you. I didn't think about the consequences of looking for their hive, but now I know what is at stake. I don't know how I can knowingly make the same decision again. It's a selfish choice, but for them to survive it might be the right one. I've thought about this a lot since I brought you down here. Our property lines span at least three miles beyond what I've found so far. As long as we keep the land and their existence a secret, they should be safe here. I can't see another way."

"Uncle Mar will want to know how I suddenly got cured," Tut challenged.

"He will," Charles replied. "You need to play sick for a while, but as long as you're with Aunt Jay, she won't let him test you or do anything you don't want him to."

His father's words were frightening to grapple with, but Tut knew they were also true.

"Dad?"

His question was cut off by the rare sound of their phone. The ringing echoed through the tunnel as clear as a bell, thanks to the baby monitor that hung off Charles' hip belt. They stared at one another, listening to the answering service and the rich tones of Helena's pre-recorded voice.

"Hi there! You've reached the Tillmans. Leave a message and we'll get back to you as soon as we can."

"Hello? Hello? Charles, I don't know if you can hear me, but Jay and I have arrived at the airport. Tut called the other day and we're both really concerned. We're headed to you now. I hope we can talk when we get there. We'll see you soon."

When the message was finished, Tut let out the breath he'd been holding. "Why do you have that baby monitor down here anyway? You never listen to our messages" he asked. I've never even seen the receiver?"

"The receiver is under your bed. It's how I monitor you when I'm down here late at night. I count your breaths and know that you're okay. It's how I keep you with me, even when it feels like we're far apart."

Charles and Tut stared at each other for a long time, seeing each other anew, before walking to the cellar door and closing it behind them, silently resolving that no matter what they did, they would do it together.

Once they reached the kitchen, they played Marrell's message again. When it was done, Charles took a seat beside his son at the kitchen table.

"Dad, what should we do?"

Charles took Tut's hand.

"I don't know Tut, but we have forty-five minutes to decide."

HUMAN

Sterling and I stood with our backs pressed so close together I could feel my sweat dampening the fabric of his shirt. The tang of fear was sharp in my mouth, but it did not overwhelm the comfort of his presence. The fact that I had an ally in this strange place I'd come to belong was a boon in and of itself. Yet I could feel the Te'Ora getting closer, like a net dropping down and closing in.

"How many did you say there were?" The rich baritone of Sterling's voice vibrated through me.

The storage car that had been our refuge swerved as the train rounded a narrow passage. The movement jostled us between the mound of luggage to our right and the jigsaw stack of wooden crates on our left. To compensate, we spread our feet a little wider.

"Two of yours. Two of mine," I whispered back.

"Okay. We need to get out of this car. If they find us first, we'll be trapped."

I nodded, hoping he would feel the movement and understand. My legs shook with the desire, the compulsion to survive. I cocked my pistol and turned my head in his direction to make sure he could hear me. "Where to?"

He faced the door to the kitchen and the dining car. I faced the passage to the servants' sleeping quarters. "This way," He grabbed my free hand and moved forward. "If they catch us, they're gonna have to do it out in the open."

The first time I saw Sterling James he was standing on the porch of the Dancing Fish, squinting against the sun behind the brim of a weathered, beaver-pelt hat. His brown eyes surveyed Union Street with a calculating ease, as if calmly weighing the odds of any number of dangerous possibilities. The main thoroughfare of Virginia City was not particularly busy that afternoon, but the fact that he *chose* to give it his undivided attention imbued everything with a significance I scarcely stopped to ponder most days. His dark beard stood clean and close against his fair complexion.

However, the fullness of his lips, the curve of his nostrils, and the way his skin held the sun's light within told me he was Black, just as I had chosen to be.

Word of the famed sheriff-turned-outlaw blew like errant dust through the town. By sundown of his first day the moniker of Sterling James could be heard in almost every corner of the city. Rumor had it that after earning a reputation as a lawman and protector of Black settlements throughout the Midwestern Territories, he retired, moving his entire family to the small town of Nicodemus, Kansas. But peace did not settle with him.

After three years of homesteading, the town members had grown fed up of paying White suppliers five times the price for the seedlings they needed to expand their livelihood. Sterling left town to negotiate a new trade arrangement with the leaders of the Cheyenne Nation and, in his absence, Nicodemus was razed to the ground by the same White suppliers who had robbed them for years. They killed almost 90 percent of the town's inhabitants, including every member of the James family. When the County Marshall refused to investigate, Sterling took matters into his own hands, forming a posse that left a trail of bodies from Grand Rapids, Michigan to as far south as San Felipe, Mexico. If the stories were true, his skill, lack of attachment, and the two guns holstered at his hip all suited my needs. Yet in the three years since I'd come here, I'd learned better than to trust my life to gossip, no matter how desperately I needed the rumors to be true.

I had to know him for myself.

Two days after his arrival, I sought him out. I rose early, expecting he would do the same, and did what I was trained to do before I lost, then found, my way. I observed him from afar while he ate his breakfast–coffee, three slices of toast, and a bowl of oatmeal sprinkled with cinnamon—on the large open porch of the Red Dog Saloon, where he'd slept the night before. Sterling was cordial, though not quite friendly, with those who approached. His left hand was never far from his pistol. A Te'Ora's sense of smell is keen, but within the confines of my human form, I struggled to make out the elements of his scent. Sandalwood soap and the steam that clung to his freshly pressed shirt mixed with the natural oils and sweat from his body to create a cologne that was both extremely masculine and utterly soothing. Unlike so many other men I'd met here, I sensed no trace of fear.

After finishing his meal, Sterling crossed the road and walked to the only Black barber in town. When he presented his nearly shaven head to Mr. Fitch, I cannot explain the comfort it gave me. I, too, had no hair before I chose the body I now inhabit.

Certain he had no knowledge of my presence, I secured my horse to the Comstock General store railing directly across from the barbershop, went inside, and hid behind three bolts of fabric, watching him.

In the thirty minutes that it took for the barber to wash and shave his scalp, Sterling never took his eyes off the door. When he walked back outside, he put on his hat, turned his head, and stared right at me before heading back across the street.

I smiled.

Our rhythms and frequencies were not of this place and human senses were rarely attuned to things outside their realm. But he noticed. I found myself unnerved, yet deeply impressed.

After testing the weight of gold in my pockets and the pistol strapped to my thigh, I secured the fastening on my traveling cloak and stepped fully into his line of sight.

Unease grew in my already crowded belly. Despite my best efforts to shield myself, I knew he'd taken the full measure of me before I'd made it halfway across the street. There was nothing I could do about that. I could not go back the way I came. And so I walked right up the porch of the Saloon and directly towards him in the way I'd been told countless times was most improper.

"You're Sterling James, the lawman from Nicodemus, Kansas.

He nodded. I took a steadying breath.

"I need an escort to accompany me on the 4:10 train to Carpinteria, Morro Bay."

"How far along are you?" His voice rippled through me like the final notes of whale song echoing off the ocean floor. The instinct to trust him was almost immediate. I tried not to.

Resisting the urge to run my hands over my belly, I met his eyes calmly. "That's none of your concern."

"It is if my job is to keep you both safe."

"Seven months," I lied. He looked at me doubtfully, as if he knew better.

"I'm carrying low. The midwife says it's a girl."

"And how many are after you?"

I feigned surprise. "Who says anyone's after me?"

Sterling's thick brows drew together in reproach as if the stupidity of my question didn't deserve an answer. I wasn't used to someone being on to me so quickly.

"Ma'am, I don't play games and I can't abide anything less than the truth. If you want my services, you're going to have to be straight with me—all the way."

Sweat dampened the back of my neck. My eyes shifted to the Saloon behind us. Gus McKenzie, manager and head barkeep of the Red Dog, alongside several of the day's patrons, was already boring a hole through the thin glass windowpanes just to get a good look at us. Sterling was already a curiosity. Me talking to him in front of company in broad daylight could easily fuel a week's worth of gossip throughout the entire town, which was exactly the kind of attention I needed to avoid. I turned back to find him studying me, waiting for my reply.

"How much would you charge to retain your services?"

"*If* I take the job, twenty-five dollars a day, plus food and lodging."

The concept of money had been one of the hardest things to grasp. I averted my eyes, silently recounting the value of the coins in my pockets. The journey would take five days. With seven-hundred dollars in gold I could afford twice as much as he charged and still have more than enough to hire a midwife for the baby when my time came.

"I accept."

"I haven't decided," he replied, but his body shifted a little closer.

I gave him my best smile. "But I have. Would you join me for dinner, Mr. James? I can give you the details you require."

He looked me over one last time before offering his

arm. I took it eagerly, feeling his strength and noting that he did not flinch at the unnatural heat of my touch. Inside the Red Dog, I requested a private dining room. What I needed to tell him was not for the faint of heart and if he was going to bolt, I'd rather he did it through the private exit than be seen storming through the main parlor.

I ordered tea and a bowl of corn chowder. He ordered a steak dinner medium rare.

"Will all your meals be this extravagant?" I asked, already counting down the expenses to come.

"This dinner is on me. I haven't decided to take you on, but until then I am a gentleman." He paused. "You should eat something, by the way, you look a bit skinny for a woman nine months into her term." He called to the waiter, "Bring another steak for her, too. Thank you, kindly."

My mouth hung open. "How could you know that?"

"I… had five sisters," he replied. "All of them had babies." Though his heartbeat spiked and sputtered, his face remained placid, a mask of control. He reached for the rolls between us and kept his gaze on buttering his bread. I reached for one as well, then tore it in half.

"Why don't you tell me about the men pursuing you?"

"Well, I killed one already." This earned his full attention. He placed his half-eaten roll and the butter knife neatly on its plate. "They'll most likely send more."

"And how did you manage to kill one of these men?"

"With a frying pan mostly—and this." I pulled out the pistol from between my thighs and placed it on the table. It was only partially true, but I didn't think he'd believe the part about me strangling a grown man with my bare hands.

Mr. James nodded his approval. "How long ago was this?"

"Yesterday morning. I can't stay here any longer. I need to leave as soon as possible before they suspect he's gone."

"And who exactly is *they*?"

Now there's the question I'd hoped to avoid. I'd lied to him two times already. There was no reason to think I could keep doing that and secure his services. He was entertaining my offer. That was apparent by the ease with which he engaged in his rather large expensive meal, but while he might be looking for a job, he wasn't desperate enough to take the first one he was offered. He had time to turn me down. Telling him I was a being from a world his people hadn't even discovered yet was not likely to build my case.

"It's a complicated situation, Mr. James."

"I'm sure it is, Ms.?"

"Moonkind. Stella Moonkind." His eyebrows raised.

I continued. "The Paiute who... helped me when I first arrived in town gave me that name. I prefer it to my family name."

Sterling nodded patiently, his eyes expectant, penetrating. I had the strange sense that he already knew what I was going to say. And even though that was impossible, I decided then and there that I would not lie to him again.

Two waiters appeared with our steaks, still sizzling with fat and butter on the plate, then left almost as quickly and silently as they came. Sterling immediately began methodically cutting his steak into thin strips. My mouth watered in appreciation. We don't eat the flesh of other beings where I'm from, but if the Te'Ora had any idea that a piece of meat could smell this delicious, I doubt there would be a single creature left alive on the entire planet.

"Please continue, Ms. Moonkind."

"Oh yes, well. The people after me are a part of my family. Their intent is to bring me home."

"A woman in your condition might find comfort in the support when the baby comes. A child needs a family to help take care–"

"No!" I blurted out. "I'll be her family and I'm sure I will be able to take care of her well enough on my own once I'm healed from the birth."

Sterling held his knife and fork aloft and studied me more closely.

"So the father is not involved."

"No," I replied, biting into a delicious strip of steak. I could taste the grass the cow ate in the way the iron in the meat surged through my blood. I closed my eyes and groaned in pleasure until the sound of Sterling's fork clattering onto the filigreed plate broke my revelry. "Are you all right?" I asked still enjoying the buttery salt of the meat juices on my tongue.

Sterling cast his eyes down, picked up his utensils once more and cleared his throat. "Why don't you want to find the child's father? Was the relationship not advantageous?"

"Oh no, you misunderstand. There was no relationship. I only met him once. He was very handsome with a powerful build, like yours. I only meant to sample him. The baby was an unexpected gift from our encounter."

Sterling looked so shocked, I couldn't help but smile. I was, of course, aware of the gender norms within this strange culture, the many things women were not supposed to talk about or do even though all the women I knew did these things anyway, with men as their willing and lustful accomplices. Because of these inconsistencies, I'd deemed these norms more a pact of secrecy than any binding agreement on conduct.

I was also aware of the effect my directness might cause, but the way he looked at me did delicious things to my nerves.

"I see," he continued. "Well then, what can you tell me about the men sent after you? How capable are they? I don't know if you killing one was due to your skill or their incompetence. I assume we can expect no more than two or three coming, but I'd like to get a sense of what I'm dealing with."

I stared at him, perplexed. "I understand, but... how do you know there are only two or three coming?"

"Because I'm sure your family has vastly underestimated your resolve to pursue your own path."

For the third time that day, my lips bent into a smile. "They will be highly trained and... adaptable." Sterling frowned, catching on quickly to my choice of words.

"Adaptable how?"

"They can change their appearance..."

His frown lines deepened. "Like a disguise?"

"Yes, except more precise. They can take on the shape and look of anyone they choose."

"You mean like actors in a play?"

"No." I took a deep breath, filling the moment and

my lungs with the dusty, life-filled air I'd come to treasure.

"Their skin. Hair. Height. Everything about them can change to blend in to their surroundings."

I watched Sterling press back against his chair, but he did not break my gaze, not for one second. "Ms. Moonkind, you are in the company of an adult. I took you for a serious woman. My time is too valuable to be taken up with fairytales."

"So is mine, Mr. James. May I remind you it is *I* who will be paying my hard-earned money to you. I would not do so if the threat were not real."

"Madam, what you suggest is not humanly possible."

I tore myself away from another tender morsel of beef to face him squarely. "No, it isn't. The threat that faces us is not one of your own."

He paused. "Whose then?"

"Mine."

His hand slid from the table and rested on his lap. I wondered at its position until I remembered his guns were still holstered at his hip.

"You look too grounded to be claiming kin to some shape-changing bounty hunters from another world, Ms. Moonkind."

I could see the moment his mind latched on to the significance of my name. His eyes flickered towards the two windows on our right, then the private exit door to our left, already calculating the threat.

Yes. He'll do nicely. More relieved than logic would dictate, considering I had a deadly pistoleer armed and seated in front of me, I continued: "That's part of what makes the beings after me so effective."

"But you claim to be one of them. If you can change as you say they can, prove it." There was no tremor in his voice as he watched me but the fine sheen of moisture that clung to his clean scalp told his true apprehension, as if he was terrified his fears might come true.

"I can't. The transformation could kill the baby. I won't risk it." I rested my hand on the swell of my belly. I did not yet know if she would be like me, but I knew I needed to remain stable until she was ready to come forth. "If she is Te'Ora, like me, she will change into the first form she is able to master, and we will live far away from your people and mine."

"So you're an alien. That's what you're telling me."

"That's what I said."

His eyes narrowed. "Does your kind study a culture before you choose it? Who you're going to be, I mean?"

"Of course."

Sterling leaned forward, raking his eyes over me with suspicion. I could see him holding his next question back, as if asking it would condemn him to believing me or reveal that he already did.

"All right then," he began. His eyes flickered around the room before they were pulled back to me. "Then I have to know, if you could be anything, look any way at all, why would a person from another planet choose to be a Black woman in these times? When things are so hard for people who look like me? There were easier choices you could've made."

"You think so?"

"Read the paper, Ms. Moonkind. It's not a secret that colored folk aren't valued highly in this land."

The sudden heaviness of his heart drew me closer. I pressed my body into the table. If I could be sure he wouldn't run away, I would've closed the distance between us and comforted him with the warmth of my own body. *He must be thinking of his family*, I realized. *All those he has lost.*

"I have lived for many centuries, Mr. James. In my experience, what a society values is not always what is most important. Your world is not the only one that has made the choice to wrap cruelty in righteousness, but my kind is not distracted by bigotry. I find my form well-suited for my purposes."

"And what is your purpose, Ms. Moonkind?"

I smiled, thinking of how much I had changed from since I arrived. I cut a slice of beef from my plate, put it into my mouth, and chewed slowly, savoring the decid-edly human experience. "My purpose has changed."

"How so?"

"My kind, the Te'Ora, seek to experience each world fully. In order to do so we choose members of society who have cultivated the ability to determine their own destinies, to make a life for themselves in every way. They must have the means to procure the necessities of survival—food, shelter, work if necessary. While self-defense is always permissible in unpredictable places, we also seek to do no harm within each world we travel."

"You could've done all those things as a White man," Sterling challenged bitterly.

I shifted closer. "Do you truly believe that? That has not been my observation. Most White men in this time seem to either be fixated on taking the resources of others or wishing they could. Those with means oppress those without, within their own community and beyond. There are, of course, exceptions, but even the youngest are indoctrinated to be this way quite thoroughly. Our kind would never be party to such aggression. However, it's not just White men who seem confined. From what I've observed, men in general do mostly what they are expected to do. They exist within a very rigid hierarchy with little room for reflection or variation in personal expression. You have your physical dominance, of course, and lead with that whenever possible, yet it seems a rather oppressive state of being.

"Women, on the other hand, are creatures of will, Mr. James! Despite men hovering over them almost constantly, women do what they want, even if they must convince themselves that it is their own desire. Only women create life. Only a woman can conquer a room full of men without a single bullet, with only the cut of her gown and the cunning in her smile. A woman must use her mind and her muscle at all times just to stay alive. I fell in love instantly and set myself to understanding all the things that women know."

"But you are a woman." Sterling replied. I could smell his growing confusion and anxiety, but I couldn't stop talking. It felt too joyous to finally share all my discoveries with someone.

"I was not born a woman, Mr. James. This is my first time." Taking in Sterling's shock, I explained. "Where I'm from there is no gender. No sex. Because we are immortal beings, there is no need to procreate. But when I came here, I chose the form of a woman because their gender seemed to have both the most fun and the most power."

"You might have found a White woman's life easier."

I frowned in confusion. "For them, it seems even worse. Not all worlds or species have 'gender' as you define it here, Mr. James, but I must say I find this world's limitations of females in general and White women in particular... to be quite perplexing. How would I function within a cohort where acquiring the means to feed myself is considered shameful? Where the very act of dressing myself without assistance is considered a hardship? To be trapped in a house all day would not afford me the opportunity to explore the world I wish to inhabit, Mr. James."

I grabbed my third roll, buttering it vigorously as I continued.

"A Black woman's life is hard, it's true, but because this society has given them no place, they have been forced to define themselves and in doing so have acquired the skills necessary to thrive on their own terms. There is *power* in that, Mr. James. Don't you find?"

There were tears in his eyes when I finally looked up.

"My sisters were that way. My momma, too."

"Of course they were," I replied, swallowing my own tears at the sound of his sorrow. "They had to be."

Silence settled between us while I gave Sterling the time he needed to collect himself.

"And what is your purpose now, Ms. Moonkind?" he asked finally.

"Freedom," I replied. "I need you to help me secure freedom for me and my daughter."

Sterling looked out the window in our private room, clearly looking for a reason to escape. "It's unreasonable of you to expect me to believe this story, Ms. Moonkind." Yet I could smell the doubt waning from his scent.

"You already sense there is something different about me."

He avoided my gaze. "That could mean anything. I hardly think that proves you're from another planet."

"Close your eyes." His gaze flickered to the revolver at the side of my half eaten roll, then back to me. "I need your help. Why would I shoot you?"

"I thought you were sane, but now I'm not so sure."

The tablecloth was as smooth as silk as I slid the gun over to him, making sure not to touch his skin. "You can hold it if you like."

He relaxed the moment his right hand closed around the barrel, then closed his eyes.

"Inhale deeply. Tell me what you smell."

He complied without hesitation. "Our dinner." His voice dropped as he searched his senses. The flare of his nostrils was subtle, but distinct like his scent, his style of dress, and the outline of muscle beneath his jacket. I knew that I was attracted to him, but I would not guess how much until later.

"The dust in the air," he continued. "The lilac and vanilla in your perfume."

"What else?"

"An energy... like the taste of lightning in the air before a storm." His lips parted and I watched his tongue hover between the perfect rows of his teeth to taste me. My hand settled over his, feeling the bones beneath his skin and the hard metal of the gun beneath that. The current of attraction was exquisite, a small bright tremor between us. I wanted him to feel that first, before I pushed my energy into him. I did not mean to release it fully, but I could not resist the echo of his heartbeat racing inside my chest.

His eyes flew open. "What the..." His body flinched back, but I held him firmly.

"I feel you... inside of me," he whispered.

"What you taste, what you feel—it's more than my attraction to you. It is the energy that allows my kind to change, to take any form and live for a very long time."

His eyes widened, looking from his stomach to mine. "Is that... the child?"

"She's moving."

For an instant, raw emotion washed over his face like a wave crashing down, only to recede, leaving an unreadable mask in its wake.

"Mr. James?"

"Release me."

Reluctantly, I let him go, held my breath, and waited

for his rejection. In my brief time here I had learned how unkind humans could be to the unfamiliar. Instead his eyes searched me, seeking answers. I did not look away. In that moment, my entire body flushed as I realized how desperately I wanted him to believe me, to know who I was, but I could not let myself be distracted from my truest cause.

"I do not expect you to believe me, Mr. James nor do I require you to. I aim to purchase your protection, not your empathy. I'll pay double to retain your services and see us safely to Carpentaria. The rest is truly none of your concern."

"The child. It's the first of your kind. That's why they want it."

I smiled at how quickly he put the pieces of me together.

"Yes. As I said, among us there is no need to procreate. I don't know how my daughter came to be, but it's never happened before in all our millennia of traveling the galaxy. But she is *mine* and I will not give her up."

Sterling sat quietly for several moments. "I don't know what you are," he said finally. "But I believe you are in danger. I stand by the price I gave you earlier. If we are in agreement, I'll take you wherever you need to go."

I felt so grateful I could barely speak.

"Thank you, Mr. James."

"Don't thank me 'til we get there, but in the meantime, please, call me Sterling."

"The fact that you can sense them is good. That means they won't be able to sneak up on you if we get separated."

Sterling's gaze snapped back from his view of the kitchen through the luggage car window. When we passed through the same room earlier, nothing seemed askew, but that was twenty minutes ago. I knew the exact time because my protector checked his watch every five minutes. He'd checked it three times before, with his fingers already edging toward the vest pocket that held his timepiece.

"We're not getting separated," he stated. "Just stay close." His determination comforted me, but I couldn't help but wonder if it would be enough to save us. We were already in more danger than I'd planned for. We boarded the train to Carpentaria without incident. Sterling arranged for the porter to carry our luggage to the storage car while I searched the passengers for any trace of the faint blue aura that no one else could see but me.

At first, there was nothing except the bristling of other First-Class passengers as we passed. *They* were incensed by the presence of two Negroes in their privileged surroundings. *We* paid them no mind and settled into our private compartment with a deep sigh, grateful for the brief respite. Though the child would mask my scent and aura from the Te'Ora, it did not guarantee our safety.

We knew they were coming.

We did not expect there to be four.

They came on horseback, posing as lawmen led by two humans who must have taught them how to do such a thing. With our curtains drawn to keep prying eyes away, we were mostly hidden from view; as were all the passengers in First Class, which is why Sterling insisted that we purchase the more expensive passage.

"Stop the train!" a sallow man in dirty chaps bellowed. "This here's the Marshall!" He turned on his horse, pointing to a portly rider dressed in a dusty black trench coat and trousers, with a silver star shining bright against the dim sky of a soiled lapel. The Marshall looked bleary-eyed and sweaty under the low brim of his hat. In a misguided effort to convey an air of authority, he raised a hand from his horse's reins and attempted some sort of salute towards the conductor. When the horse shifted, the Marshall nearly fell over.

Red-faced with embarrassment, the leader of their crew turned from the Marshall and addressed the train conductor once more. "You got a fugitive hiding in there and we got a right to board this train!" His left hand was held high, waving a wanted poster with a crude likeness of me etched on the front. Behind him, my kin waved similar posters like flags.

Despite the severity of the circumstances, I couldn't help a chuckle. The description for my likeness must have been pale and round. The drawing resembled more of what I looked like in my natural state interpreted through the lens of someone who'd never known anything beyond human physiology. I watched as the leader of their party and both Te'Ora boarded the coach side of the train, while the Marshall clung to his horse, seemingly happy to let the others do the hard work on his behalf.

It was never Sterling's plan for us to stay in our private quarters to be quietly murdered and then disposed of. As soon as they boarded, we slipped out of our carriage suite, heading through the dining car to the kitchen two cars down. From there we made our way to the luggage hold. We took our time, gathering extra ammunition and solidifying our plans to survive. With a cautious nod my way, Sterling walked back through the kitchen and opened the door.

The dining car, which had been almost empty twenty minutes ago, was now filled to the brim. Along the periphery, waiters hastily filled trays with libations to bring back to anxious guests in First Class. At the center of the ruckus more waiters expertly navigated through a throng of angry passengers. Businessmen and their wives, performers and merchants, all venting their outrage in escalating tones while demanding to know what the good manager of the Pullman train planned to do about this disruption.

"We don't know anything about the fugitive," the conductor's assistant explained. "Our porters assure us there's no one on this train that matches their description."

Once the swinging doors settled behind me, the smell of spirits and sweat was stifling. But above it all, hanging in a noxious plume of white smoke, was something worse.

"Do you think we should risk trying to move past?" I whispered. Sterling squeezed my hand and pulled me forward. Skimming the edge of the room, we managed to stay mostly unnoticed, save a few errant scowls by two members of the elite and racist. But that was not my biggest problem. At the opposite end of the room, at the back of the crowd, was a man who stood with a large, white mustache twitching like a cat's whiskers. He had something brown, long, and wet protruding from his lips.

"That *smell*." I groaned. My stomach clenched in a way I knew well from the first few months of carrying the baby. Any minute, I feared I would purge.

"Cigar smoke," Sterling replied before turning his full attention on me. "It's making you sick."

I nodded, too scared to open my mouth and invite my insides out. He squeezed my hand, then turned his gaze towards the exit. "Just a little bit closer. Hold on. It'll clear up as soon as we..."

Consumed with the task of managing my own nausea, it took me a moment to notice that Sterling's voice had trailed off, but I wasn't alarmed until he stopped moving altogether. My queasiness was immediately replaced by the stillness of fear.

"Ms. Moonkind, step behind me and draw your weapon."

Following his gaze, I saw the source of our peril. Two bounty hunters, one human, one Te'Ora, staring at us from across the room.

"I thought you'd agreed to call me Stella," I joked. The tension had the odd effect of making me slightly giddy, which was not an emotion I had experienced before, but then again neither was the fear of dying. The notion that I could be funny startled me. I let out a short burst of laughter.

"How likely are they to open fire in a crowd?" Sterling asked, rightfully ignoring me. I glanced down to find both his pistols cocked and ready at his side.

"Normally, we would not risk it, but I don't imagine

that normal considerations apply," I whispered back. "They will do what is necessary to get the child."

"They do realize they can't have the baby without taking you with them—alive?"

"I'm not sure that has occurred to them."

Sterling's response was to press his body closer to mine. I pulled my pistol out from the pocket of my skirt, holding the firearm in my right hand while my left arm wrapped around his waist.

We don't have names where I come from, at least none that can be pronounced with human vocal chords, but if we did, I would name the bounty hunters they sent to kidnap me something akin to Slick and Cold. I could sense their consciousness, like a worm eating through my faith in our survival. Without a moments hesitation for the harm they would cause, the first Te'Ora grabbed one of the kerosene lanterns that hung above the bar and threw it into the crowd. Oil spilled onto the tables and floor and quickly caught fire. For a moment, my view of them was obscured by the rush of men and women scattering like fleas from a beaten rug. The fire spread, leaping from one table to another, and for a moment, I could not look away. There is nothing like fire at home, nothing that gives off such seductive heat.

"Great God."

The sound of Sterling's soft gasp drew my attention, forcing my eyes back to the threat before us.

The second Te'Ora had arrived and with one common purpose, the husks of their human bodies began to pull away. Their lone human companion stumbled back in surprise as the faces of the men he thought he knew stretched out, taking up twice the size of any normal human head until it settled into the wide, oblong shape of my people. Their skin, once riddled with stubble and pock marks, turned from ruddy pale to translucent pink. The small ears that hung from the side of their heads split into three tendrils that could both hear every sound better than any human could hope to and taste the surrounding air. Hundreds of delicate cilia sprouted from the lining of each tentacle ensuring that the slightest movement would not go unnoticed.

Powerful arms stretched through the leather of their worn jackets until webbed hands hung far past their cuffs and thick webbed toes burst from the seams of their boots.

"What the hell is going on here?" their human companion bellowed. But the poor man would never get a chance to find out. The second Te'Ora raised a long, webbed finger and pulled the trigger of their gun, putting a bullet through his left eye.

Sterling grew dangerously still while I shuddered, rattled by the sight of my kin acting in cold-blood.

I'd never seen another of our kind in true form outside of the dark waters of our home. With the fire raging between us making everything dry and hot and the sky a broad stroke of pale sapphire rushing past our moving train, they looked truly out of place. Though in truth I had no more right to be here than they did. I was still an imposter hiding my true nature under my ability to mimic other life.

Yet, I *felt* different.

I had traveled many worlds, shaping myself to the environment so that I might go unnoticed as I observed the universe, but never had I wanted to be seen until I came here. Whether I belonged or not no longer mattered. From the moment I smelled the hot air and opened my eyes to the beauty of this place, I understood. All my life I had been trying on other people's lives, other people's bodies, until finally I found the one shape that defined—not who I had been, but who I wanted to become. A person. A *she*. A woman.

My eyes stung gazing at the embodiment of all I had been. I did not belong here either, but I wanted to desperately. To become myself at last.

"Te'Ora, give us the offspring and we will leave you to your fate." Their voices betrayed only a hint of anger, but I could sense their essence burning, alight with rage.

The heat from the fire was becoming almost unbearable, consuming the space between us. Beside me, Sterling's face was now covered with the bandana he wore around his neck, frantically searching for an exit.

"We are inseparable, Te'Ora," I replied. Their eyes narrowed, searching our connection for a trace of untruth they would not find. With no real understanding of the mechanics of gestation, the thought that I could not simply hand my child over had not occurred to them.

"Then you will come with us."

Because our vocal cords are not shaped in the same way that humans' are, speech outside of water is different. Instead of the fluid ribbon of sounds that make up the language patterns of human speech, our language is more like a series of clicks, almost too low for human ears to perceive. So I did not expect Sterling to react when they spoke.

Yet, in an instant, Sterling was between us, shielding my body with his and two guns pointed at my kin.

"She's not going with you."

His voice was quiet, yet there was no mistaking the certainty in it. Relieved, I inhaled and immediately began choking on the smoke. My kin stared back at Sterling, puzzled.

"Does the human understand us?"

Until that moment we'd spoken in our native language, but I replied in English, refusing to isolate Sterling any more than he already was. With a pang of regret, I realized that in my fixation to protect my child, I had placed him in danger. As capable as Sterling was, he was also outnumbered. The only human in a room full of aliens.

"I don't know, but he senses more than most."

"Regardless, he is not Te'Ora. We must protect our own."

"I am no longer one of you."

Their tendrils twitched in confusion. "You have formed another union?"

I could feel the skepticism as they glanced between Sterling and I. They sensed our connection, the unconscious need to be near one another, but it was not a bond they understood. It was nothing like the bond of our species. There was too much emotion, too much heat, too much uncertainty. The pair of Te'Oras looked at one another.

"No," I replied. "I belong only to myself." There is no word for *alone* in our language. No concept of "self" as something that exists outside of the whole.

"You cannot break with us," they replied, struggling to even to find the words.

I'm trying to, I thought.

"I already have," I said, stepping closer to Sterling seeking the strength and courage his proximity inspired in me.

"How strong are your kind?" Sterling whispered.

"Stronger than yours."

"So don't get in a tussle?"

"Not if you can help it."

"Got it."

Sterling fired well before I saw him move or registered the "t" in the last syllable he uttered. The echo from the first crack of gunfire drowned out the next seven shots he'd made, square and true before my kin could fire back.

With four hits to the chest each, they shouldn't have been able to fire back, but after a moment of clear distress, they did. Luckily, Sterling was faster, kicking over a table for us to hide behind. He pulled me to the ground beside him.

"So, bullets don't penetrate," he said, obviously dismayed by the effect his perfect aim seemed to lack.

"Not at that range. The impact slows us down a bit, but we spend most of our time underwater. You develop a tough skin."

"I thought you said you killed one of them with *that* pistol."

"The pistol helped, but I had to take them down with a cast-iron skillet, then strangle them with the hem of my skirt." Sterling turned his attention from the fire and the hail of bullets. For one brief, incredulous second, he looked at me.

"You didn't tell me I needed a skirt," he replied before firing another round across the slim distance between us. I thought I saw the sliver of a smile pull at the corner of his mouth, but it was gone before I had the chance to be sure. "Regardless, I hadn't planned on getting that close."

I opened my mouth to speak, but my thoughts dissolved in the sudden silence that surrounded us. Beside me, Sterling pulled back the hammer on the revolver in his left hand, holstered the second gun at his hip, then grabbed my arm. "We need to move. Now."

The Te'Ora must've had the same idea because before we could hit our stride, they launched themselves over the table, hurling toward us. Sterling took the brunt of the attack, pushing me out of the way just before the impact propelled him clear across the room. Both Te'Ora would have landed on top of him if he didn't roll away at the last moment. Still, he was too close to get away from them.

While one of my kin shrieked in pain from an awkward landing, the other grabbed Sterling's shin, pulling him closer. Sweat soaked his forehead and shirt as he fought to escape, but there was too much blood running down the side of his face. Without some reprieve, I knew he would not make it. I scrambled to right myself. With my body so fully distended, it was difficult to maneuver but I got to my knees and crawled toward the closest of my kin who was rising from the ground and headed toward Sterling. With their attention turned away, they did not see me lurch forward. I caught them by the cuff of their worn trousers and sat back, pulling with every ounce of fury I felt until their body came crashing down. Just ahead, Sterling was still on his back, but using his free leg to kick the other Te'Ora in the face and shoulders, his blows hard and steady. It did not seem to loosen their grip, but it did slow their progression, which was enough for now to keep him alive.

I surrendered most of my strength in undergoing the process that allowed me to transform and retain my human shape, but I was still physically stronger than the average human. The Te'Ora, however, had changed back to their original forms, clearly hoping to leverage their natural advantage. However, I planned to use something else entirely; something I had learned from my time here on earth.

Pain was not something we experienced often. On

our world, as immortal beings, we have no predators. An accident or profound sickness were generally the only ways that we experienced death or separation from one another. Time had made us strong. Our connection as one mind made us efficient, with no purpose or compulsion beyond our collective survival and advancement. But we were weak in other ways. Without personal interest, a singular thought to call your own, your insides stay as empty as a cavern holding nothing but the echo of other voices. Te'Ora never develop the inner layers of thought that harden and fill the inner space with dreams, cravings, *desires* that grow and crystalize into the strongest thing I have ever known: the will to want—the will to survive when your very next breath is not promised.

I could see it in Sterling's eyes as he fought against a strength twice his own and held it back. And I brought that same will down upon my kin as I grabbed a broken wine glass from the floor and sank its ragged edge deep into the thin flesh between my kin's ankle and large, webbed feet. I pulled it out and stabbed them again as they succumbed to their pain, until I was sure they would not get up.

It was an awful thing that I did. Calculated and cruel. I knew the vulnerability of their physiology as well as my own

Yet instead of horror, I felt a cold, certain satisfaction. I was safe. My child was safe and us, not "them," was what I set my will to. My kin stared up at me with a fist clutched tight to their chest. Tears of anguish fell from their eyes, seeing me for the first and last time not as the Te'Ora that they had known for millennia, but the strange thing—not quite Te'Ora not quite human— that I had become. It took a moment for me to notice the flash of dim light between their dead fingers. My human eyes were so dull! By the time I kicked it out of their hand it was too late. The alarm on the long-range communicator had been sent—more would come soon. I crushed the device under my boot for no other reason but raw frustration and spite.

A few feet away, Sterling had ten seconds left of air before he passed out. I could hear it in his frantic heart. I could see it in his eyes as his feet hovered six inches above the ground, lifted and pressed up against the wall with Te'Ora hands around his neck, choking the life from him.

I screamed, moving towards him on legs that were not quick enough to save him. When Sterling's arms dropped to his sides I stumbled, unable to believe that he would simply give up the last few seconds of his life, until I saw the gun rise up beside my kin's right temple. By the time understanding flashed between them, Sterling had used his last breath to pull the trigger. They both fell, but I only ran to Sterling. Cradling him to my chest, I held him, startled and relieved to hear him gasping for breath.

"Close range works," he rasped before passing out entirely.

~

"Sterling!" I slapped him hard across the face, impatient for the smelling salts to work.

His eyes fluttered, but just barely. I raised my hand, prepared to strike again.

"Ma'am, please. Give him some air," the head porter scolded as he and two other Black men laid Sterling down across the seat cushion of our private carriage. I would have felt ashamed except pain was already lancing through me. The water that had spilled from my body, that everyone assumed was simply the result of fear, was something altogether different.

"I'm sorry. You're right, of course," I replied, feeling the prickling of sweat break out all over my scalp.

"Don't fret, Miss. I'm sure your husband will come right along in a minute or so. Try to calm yourself. Fighting them creatures couldn't of been easy for him. We see any more of them things, don't worry. Thanks to him, we know what to do to kill 'em on sight."

My entire body shuddered.

"But don't you worry about any of that," the porter

continued. "He wouldn't want you getting yourself all worked up in your condition. Best calm down. You don't want to have that baby right here on the train, do ya?"

Of course he wasn't really looking at me or else he would have known that I *was* having a baby on this train. Tension was taking over my body again and for the second time that day, I felt a bubble of hysteria rise up in me, waiting to explode in a fit of crazed laughter. Instead, I tamped it down, smiled meekly, and took the small jar of smelling salts he offered.

"Give him a good ten minutes before waving that under his nose again. He'll come to," the porter said with a kind smile.

"Thank you, Mr. Wells." I waited until I was sure he and his two attendants had left the first class car before I pulled the curtains and let out my first whimper. Whether it was out of true discomfort or fear, I couldn't say.

To describe what I was feeling as pain was not entirely accurate, it was more pressure with a distinct promise of pain to come. Pacing back and forth, I found myself both fascinated and terrified by the small ache that grew and grew as time passed. The urge to change form, to escape the seemingly impossible task that lay before me was powerful–almost as consuming as the desire to see this birth, this miracle, through; but not quite. I panted louder trying to use my breath as a foil for my fear.

"How far apart are your contractions?"

His voice startled me, not just because of the sound, but the unhurried tenor, too–as if he was asking for a cup of tea.

I dropped to my knees. "Are you all right?"

His smile was small, but true. "I think I'm doing better than you are right now."

"How could you know that?"

"Why wouldn't I know?"

"My water broke two hours ago in front of the entire crew of male porters and no one noticed."

"To be a good lawman you have to teach yourself to notice things that other people don't. I aim to be the best, so I guess that means I'm not like most men."

"I've noticed."

Sterling closed his eyes and smiled. "So, how far apart?"

Stella struggled to calm her mind and think back "Maybe seven minutes."

He opened his eyes in time to see my confused expression.

"Five sisters, remember? I helped them deliver each one of their babies." When my eyes got wider, he pulled himself up to a sitting position. "How much do you know of what's about to happen?"

"I know that I'm about to push seven pounds and six ounces of baby out of a very small opening."

He broke out into a smile that was full of amused assurance. "Well, that's pretty much it."

I'm sure there was more I should have known or did know, but I couldn't remember. At the time, I simply did what Sterling told me to do and at the end of a body that felt pushed to the point of breaking, a miracle emerged, with tiny pink tentacle wiggling on the sides of a little brown face that was just a shade lighter than my own chosen skin. The webbed toes and feet of the Te'Ora were there, but less pronounced with long fingers that reached up to grab Sterling's nose and pull on it with enough strength to surprise and delight him.

I'd worried that the sight of our true form might be too disturbing for Sterling to carry on with me, but instead of fear, he drew my daughter closer in pure wonder. They studied each other in silence. I watched his eyes roam and linger over the broad shape of her face. Her large, purple, lidless eyes. Her tiny nose and broad, full lips. With the sharp focus and awareness of our kind, I watched as she in turn traced her fingertips over the thick curves of his eyebrows and the moles that sat just above the edges of his beard on both cheeks. He laughed as she tickled him. By the time her fingers sank into the wiry curls of his beard, searching for the dimples that hid there, we were all laughing with an abandon that brought tears to my eyes. When my daughter turned to me, she'd already taken the color of his eyes, his mole for her right cheek, and a dimple on her left. The delicate cilia on her head were replaced with a great mound of soft, reddish-brown curls. I smiled, I cried, and I thought she was just as beautiful, wild, and wonderful as the world into which she had come.

Four days later, we arrived safely at Carpentaria. Sterling quickly became the sheriff of the small coastal town, setting up his house a short way from the ocean. Every evening he watched from the shore, waiting for his mysterious wife and daughter to return from the ocean's depths and tell him of the world below. And though the Te'Ora did return, searching for many years, they never caught the scent of Stella Moonkind or her offspring again.

ABOUT THE AUTHOR

National bestselling and award-winning author Cerece Rennie Murphy has published ten novels, children's books and short stories, including her latest release Between Two Seas. In addition, Mrs. Murphy and her son are also working on completing Ellis and The Cloud Kingdom, the 3rd book in the Ellis and the Magic Mirror early reader children's book series. Mrs. Murphy lives and writes in her hometown of Washington, DC with her family. To learn more about the author and her upcoming projects, please visit her website at www.cerecerenniemurphy.com.